HEXED DETECTIVE

M.V. STOTT

Copyright © 2018 by Uncanny Kingdom.

All rights reserved.

No part of this book may be reproduced in any form or by any electronic or mechanical means, including information storage and retrieval systems, without written permission from the author, except for the use of brief quotations in a book review.

BECOME AN INSIDER

Sign up and receive **FREE UNCANNY KINGDOM BOOKS**. Also, be the **FIRST** to hear about **NEW RELEASES** and **SPECIAL OFFERS**. Just visit:

WWW.UNCANNYKINGDOM.COM

HEXED DETECTIVE

1

As she dressed that Tuesday morning, Detective Rita Hobbes had no idea she was about to take a tumble down the rabbit hole. That life as she knew it would soon slip away and be replaced by a hidden, dangerous world. A world that lived in the shadows and tip-toed behind the known; that skulked down secret streets and lurked within whispered rooms.

No, all Rita knew when she got up that morning was that she'd drank far too much the previous night, and now her head felt like the Incredible Hulk was using it as a stress toy.

'Christ on a bike,' she groaned as she surveyed herself in the mirror. Her eyes looked as though someone had used her face as a coffee table and left behind two dark rings. 'Never again,' she said, knowing there was every chance she'd break that vow before the day was done.

She didn't have time for a shower. Instead, she sniffed at her dark red hair, then her armpits, and grimaced before grabbing a can of deodorant and spraying herself from head to toe. Having half-arsed her ablutions, she padded out of the bedroom in desperate need of about two gallons of water and a bacon sandwich.

Rita was thirty-one years of age and liked to pretend she was much happier in her thirties than she had been in her twenties. She'd lived in Blackpool her whole life, and very much hoped she didn't die there. Rita was an orphan, passed from orphanage, to foster family, and back again, multiple times. The most oft-cited reason for the termination of her foster family placements had been the biting. She had bitten *so* many people *so* many times. Not just a nibble, no, she'd sunk her teeth in right up to the gums.

And that had not been the end of her youthful rap sheet. There had also been the fires. And the stealing. And that time she'd poisoned Jason Cooper, a fellow orphan, with pellets meant for rat traps. She'd done that after he'd grassed on her for drawing a penis on Maggie Karen's forehead while she took a nap.

Rita Hobbes had been marked down as a "bad egg".

Many had feared that all that lay ahead for young Rita was a life of crime, or perhaps a spell on the women's wrestling circuit, but instead, she surprised them all by ending up on the other side of the law. Grown-up Rita hadn't wound up in jail, or face-down on the wrestling mat, instead she became a Detective Sergeant for the Blackpool Police.

Rita was stood in the kitchen of her house, gulping down her third glass of water, when she realised she wasn't home alone.

'Oh, you're still here,' she said as she turned to the kitchen table and discovered a man sat there in his underpants, eyes half-shut, hair a thick, dark bird's nest.

'Yup, still here,' agreed Chris Farmer, Rita's sort of, but not really at all, boyfriend. She'd been quite clear on the terms of their relationship: they could go to the pictures to watch a film and then talk about the film over beer and pizza afterwards. They could also have sex, should they both feel so inclined. And that was as far as it went. No emotions. No sharing. No obligations. No sleeping over. But there he was. It was morning, and there he was.

'Sorry,' he said, gnawing at a piece of toast that had clearly been left in the toaster a minute too long, 'meant to go, but I fell asleep after we had the sex. And now here we are.'

'Looks like it, yeah.'

'Don't mind, do you?'

Rita really, really did mind. Like, a lot. A more subtle soul would have put this across gently, or even pretended it was no big deal. But this was Rita Hobbes he was dealing with.

'Of course, I bloody care, Chris. You know the rules. I told you to print off the list I emailed and pin it to your fridge so you wouldn't forget.' She sat opposite him and swiped a slice of toast from his plate. 'You'll remember to go home next time, though, right?'

'Right.'

'It's not like we're bloody married.'

'Heaven forbid.'

Rita munched on the pilfered toast and spat crumbs as she spoke. 'Exactly. This is a very casual pleasure thing. As agreed. No point rocking the boat now.'

'We're on the same page,' he replied.

Rita chewed on the burnt toast as she eyeballed him. She wasn't entirely convinced that they were on the same page, or that they were, in fact, reading the same book.

'It's just... we are both very good at the sexy times business, right?' said Rita.

'No complaints here.'

'Good, so why ruin it by adding all the relationship stuff? The pretending to care about how each other's day went, the holding hands and throwing bread at stupid ducks, the his and hers matching pyjamas, and the simmering resentment. All that crap.'

'Those are your best examples of relationship things?'

'I'm telling you, a loving relationship is the best way to ruin a casual shag.'

Chris stood and took his empty plate over to the sink. 'Okay, okay, I get the message. I will never sleep over again, Scout's honour.' He checked his watch. 'Shit. Shit it. I'm going to be late. The Guv will have my balls.'

Rita watched him scamper off to retrieve his clothes from upstairs.

Rita lived in a small, two-bedroom house on a street of identical-looking houses. The rent was incredibly cheap as the place was riddled with damp, and the electrics were, at best, massively dangerous.

Still. Cheap.

People had asked why she didn't just buy a place, but buying a place meant staying in Blackpool, and that was the last thing Rita wanted.

A car horn blared outside.

'Shit.' She knew who that was. 'Chris, stay out of sight, yeah?' she called upstairs.

'I'm the phantom shagger, got it. So, are we gonna meet tonight? Rita? Hey?' Chris poked his head over the bannister and looked down just in time to see the front door closing behind Rita. 'Good idea,' he said, 'let's play it by ear.'

Rita waved a middle finger in the direction of the car parked on the opposite side of the road. The smartly-dressed man with neat sandy hair gave his car horn a further, very annoying, blast. This was DS Dan Waterson, Rita's partner, and ride to work that morning. She had a car of her own, but more often than not it stayed in the station car park due to her habit of drinking too much to drive home after work.

'When you're ready,' said Waterson, before inhaling from his e-cig and blowing a cloud of vapour out of the window.

'Why do you always have to be in on time, Waters?' asked Rita, as she yanked open the passenger door and collapsed into her seat, rocking the car.

'Because that's what time we're paid to start.'

'Teacher's pet.'

'Man hands.'

'Coffee?'

Waterson smiled and reached down, grabbing a styrofoam cup of overpriced coffee and handing it over. It was as Rita sipped the coffee that she noticed the front door to her house open, and saw Chris Farmer emerge, blinking into the morning light.

'He does not take direction,' she grumbled as Waterson spotted him and turned to her with a shit-eating grin on his face.

'Well, well, well. Is that young Chris Farmer I spy, beginning his walk of shame from your house of sin?'

'Why are you always so cheery in the morning, Waters?' Rita asked. 'It's your third most irritating trait. Why can't you be quiet and depressed like a normal person?'

'How many times do I have to ask you not to call me Waters? You know I don't like it, you know it annoys me, why do you still do it?'

'I think you just answered your own questions, Waters.'

Waterson sighed. 'Also, I thought you said you and him was a one-off?'

'It was.'

'And how many times have you enjoyed this "one-off"?'

'About fifty.'

'He's uniform,' said Waterson. 'It's like bonking the hired help. Very unseemly, Rita.'

Rita gave Waterson the finger as she slotted her seatbelt home and the car pulled away.

The stone was slate-grey, two metres in length, one in width, with rusty metal manacles affixed, ready for wrists and ankles.

The figure in the blood-red robe ran his hand across the stone's surface.

'It's time,' said the voice that only he could hear. The voice that had been with him, a constant companion, since he had been a child.

'At last,' he replied, and felt a tear run down his cheek.

2

Sometimes Jane dreamed about a man who wore a rabbit mask.

The mask was old and frayed, not made of plastic or rubber like a modern mask. No, this mask had history. Jane knew that if the strange man were to take off his mask then hand it to her, and she was to place the ratty thing over her own head, the smell from inside—ancient, rancid, an overpowering odour like despair and emptiness—would eject the contents of her stomach at once.

The dream had ghosted around inside of her sleeping mind ever since she was small. She would wake in the black with the imagined smell assaulting her twitching nose, and she would shake as though she were a dog attempting to throw off water after a frantic, deep plunge.

Often, Jane would forget what it was that had made her wake up with such an off-kilter feeling. Other times she would recall nothing more than the rabbit mask itself, or perhaps just its damp basement smell.

'Do you like my mask?'

She turned over in bed and kicked her legs.

'You're doing it again,' said Greg in a weary mumble, patting her flank with the back of one hand.

'No, I'm not.'

'Oh. Must be someone else then.'

'Do you like my mask?'

Jane smiled and turned on to her side, her back to Greg, and curled so that her knees almost touched her chest. She knew when Greg tapped her that she'd been having the rabbit mask dream, even if she couldn't remember it. Rabbit mask was the only dream that made her kick and squirm.

'Knock, knock,' said the man in the rabbit mask, *'it's time. Time to start. Time to end. Time to send you round the bend.'*

That morning, as Jane stumbled from the bed to the shower to the kitchen to the couch, she had no idea that she would never have the rabbit mask dream again. Never have any dream again.

Greg had already been up and out of bed when she woke, but she could hear him now, clattering around in the kitchen.

Jane grabbed the remote and flicked on the TV set. Static greeted her. 'Shit.' She pressed another channel. More static. 'Greg, is the telly broken?'

'No,' replied Greg. 'Everything is fine, fine, fine.'

Jane went from channel to channel, but all were gone. Finally, she discovered a channel that was working. On-screen was a close-up of what looked like a mask, fashioned into a hedgehog's head.

It made Jane's heart judder.

It wasn't the rabbit mask of her dreams, but it was clearly of the same type. Old, tatty, wrong.

Jane jabbed at the remote and the TV changed channel. The man in the hedgehog mask stared out at her. She changed the channel over and over again, but there he was, there he always was, the mask filling the screen.

As her heart boom-boomed, Jane got down on to her knees and shuffled forward on the carpet, peering closer at the hedgehog mask. It seemed to her that its wearer was returning her gaze, which, of course, was impossible.

Impossible.

Jane could hear the person breathing, in and out, in and out, raspy, harsh against the mask. She had the strange fear that if she were to move any closer towards the screen, the hedgehog man would reach out and grab hold of her.

'You shouldn't sit so close you know,' said Greg, who had entered the room behind her. 'You'll get square eyes.'

'Greg, I don't think I like this TV channel.'

'No, it's fine. It's fine, fine, fine.'

She turned from the screen to look up at her boyfriend, who smiled down at her. It was an odd sort of smile, Jane thought, but that wasn't the oddest thing about Greg. No, the oddest thing was that he didn't have any eyes. Birds had taken up home inside Greg's head, their small, sharp beaks poking out of his eye sockets.

'Oh, I enjoy this show,' said Greg, pointing to the hedgehog-masked stranger on screen. 'Do I? I think I do. I'm sure I've seen it before and before and before.'

As she listened to Greg talk, Jane realised he didn't sound much like her boyfriend at all. The voice was too flat, empty of any colour or nuance. It was like someone had hollowed out his voice, and if she were to poke one of his words with her finger as he spoke them, it would collapse in on itself.

'Who are you?' she asked.

'I am Greg. Greg your boyfriend. We have dated for years and years and rent this house at a reasonable cost, all things considered. Shall we kiss?'

'No.'

'Okay,' said Greg, and he dug into his pocket, retrieving a fist of soil full of fat, wiggling worms. 'Everything is fine,

fine, fine.' He began to pull worms from the soil clump and hold them before his eye sockets, the beaks snapping hungrily until one found its target and pulled the worm from his fingers and hauled it into his head.

Jane wondered how he could see her with his eye sockets full of beaks. How could he think at all with a skull stuffed with feathers and talons and sharp, hungry squawks? She stood and began to edge away from Not Greg, as she now thought of him. Not Greg with his dead voice and his starving beak eyes.

'Where are you going?' asked Not Greg, feeding fat worm after fat worm to the snapping beaks.

'Nowhere.'

'Oh, that's not true. That's not true at all,' said Not Greg as she edged around the room, moving slowly toward the door. Not Greg turned from her, back to the TV set. 'Ah yes, I do remember this show, I knew I did. This is the Mr. Spike show. Mr. Spike is funny, you know. Or terrifying. Or silly. Something along those lines.'

Jane was three steps from the door, her eyes never leaving Not Greg as he stood transfixed by the non-moving person in the mouldy hedgehog mask.

'Once I met Mr. Spike on a road that didn't exist. He took off his mask and I pulled out my eyes so as not to see what was shown. I can laugh about it now, you know. Everything is funny, given time.'

A beak pierced the back of Not Greg's head and wiggled and fought until the bird's entire head poked through slick with gore, and stared at Jane with black, blank eyes.

She ran from the room.

From the house.

From Not Greg and his head full of birds.

From the man in the hedgehog mask.

She raced for her car and started the engine, stomping

the accelerator and leaving her house behind, but she found that the sound of the man in the hedgehog mask's breathing remained. Rough and guttural, constant and steady, as though he was in the passenger seat, leaning over, his masked face centimetres from her ear. Jane felt as though she could feel his hot, damp breath on her face, smell the rancid air blowing from his lungs, landing damp and sticky upon her skin. It made her feel like she wanted to lean away, even though the car was empty. Like she wanted to turn her head and gag.

It was just another dream, that's all. She thought she'd woken up, but she hadn't, not really. That had to be the truth of it, because real life wasn't like this.

Or perhaps she'd gone mad.

It was all very strange and unreal, and it made Jane feel all shaky on the inside, as though her organs were bashing into each other like pinballs. Going batty had always been one of her greatest fears. Some yelped at spiders scuttling, others trembled deep down at the very idea of travelling by aeroplane, but the worry that sneaked up on Jane in her darker times was the fear of losing her marbles.

'Who are you, then?' her Granddad Thomas would say when she went to visit him in those final few years.

'It's me Granddad, Jane, your granddaughter,' she would reply, softly.

'Oh? Oh no. No, I don't think so, love. I'm only twenty-two, I haven't even had kids yet,' and he would look down at his wrinkled, brown-spotted hands in confusion.

'You're not mad, or dreaming, not at all,' said a man sitting calmly on the back seat of the car.

He wore a rabbit mask.

The wheel turned sharply and the car tyres screamed in complaint as the world lurched round and round, until things came to a sudden stop and Jane bashed her head painfully against the door window and things turned into fuzz and sparks.

'My name is Mr. Cotton. I believe you recently met my good brother, Mr. Spike.'

Her world tilting, Jane fumbled at the seat belt with rubber fingers.

'Look at you now,' said Mr. Cotton, 'all grown up and ready for the chop. The first of a bad batch.'

Free of her seat belt, Jane pushed open the door and stumbled out of the car, now resting diagonally with a rear wheel up on the pavement. Her hands scuffed the ground as she made her escape, painting the tarmac red.

'Where are you going, Jane? It's time. Your time. He's waiting for you. Rude to be late.'

Jane had felt scared many times in her life.

There was the time she was six and her dad had taken her to the local swimming baths. She'd thought she knew what she was doing, but soon enough she'd walked too far, and under she went, knowing there was no way she'd be able to get above the water again to catch her breath—

There were the times in class when the teacher was going from pupil to pupil and she knew she was going to have to stand and speak in front of everyone and her mouth was so, so dry and her heart was fluttering—

There was the time she climbed over a fence to retrieve a ball, and just as she found it and picked it up she heard a low growl and turned to see the biggest dog that had ever been, baring its fangs, head down, drool pouring, and the fence was too far away and there was no way she was going to make it but she turned to run anyway—

But this wasn't like that, this was a deep-down terror, primal and old and undeniable. It was *other* and it was *wrong* and it was *inevitable*. It was where she'd always been headed.

Jane felt like curling up into a ball and crying.

Hexed Detective

Instead, she ran.

Ran down streets she didn't recognise, which she knew was impossible, because she knew every street in Blackpool like the back of her hand. She'd lived her entire life in the same faded seaside town, clinging to the west coast of England, shaking hands with the sea. And yet turn after turn took her deeper into confusion.

'Just one thing, just show me one thing I know,' but the strange and the new were all that she found.

This wasn't her home. This wasn't her town. She was lost and she was going to have to stop running because her body couldn't stand another step. Half crouching, half falling, she reached out to cushion the blow as she dropped to the ground and tore at the air with great, ragged breaths.

'There you are. I've been waiting for you.'

She looked up to see the man in the rabbit mask stood before her.

'You're not real,' said Jane. 'You're just a nightmare. You're not real!'

'It's true, I am a nightmare, but I am also very real. My name is Mr. Cotton, and this is my dear brother, Mr. Spike.'

The man from the television, the man in the hedgehog mask, stepped in beside him.

'What do you want?' Jane begged.

'I told you. It's time. The Magician is waiting.'

And then Mr. Spike took off his mask.

3

The man had been running for a long, long time.

It had started on the Underground—on the Piccadilly line—as the train shot rat-a-tat and shaky through the dark. His plan had been to change at Green Park, hop on to the Victoria line, and head for Oxford Circus.

The carriage was crammed with people heading towards the always crowded shopping hub of London, and the man was stood gripping a bar, uncomfortably close to a cluster of strangers. Normally, the close proximity of a hygienically-challenged man's ripe armpit would have driven him to distraction, but he had far worse things demanding his attention today.

He thought he'd been discreet, but Carlisle had discovered what he'd done.

He'd been drinking at The Beehive pub, sure his secret was safe when an extremely unpleasant eaves who went by the name of Razor had delighted in telling him that his secret was, in fact, public knowledge. It seemed Razor had sold him out for a taste of magic, ratted on him to someone he knew who would pass on the information to Carlisle's ears.

Hexed Detective

The man had abandoned his two-thirds-full drink and fled the pub in search of sanctuary. Carlisle knew that the man had told the London Coven about what he'd been up to, and Carlisle was not the sort to let that go.

The man knew people on Oxford Street, people who could squirrel him away, undetected. He had a feeling that he'd have to stay hidden a good long while; it was said that Carlisle had been known to nurse grudges for centuries. He was hopeful that he'd been tipped off early enough to make it into his hidey-hole. More than hopeful.

He was three stops from Green Park when things started to go wrong.

The train lurched to a stop at Gloucester Road and belched up its passengers, who shoved their way out of the carriage before the waiting horde bundled on to the train after them, staking a claim to whatever small space they could find.

The man had a beanie hat pulled down so it almost covered his eyes, and was doing his best not to catch anyone's attention. Travelling on the underground was a dangerous gambit he knew, eyes were everywhere, but it was also the quickest way to get where he needed to be. So he'd taken the risk, shrinking under his hat and hiding within the folds of his large overcoat.

Over and over in his head, he repeated the mantra: *see me not, see me not, see me not*. It was a weak type of perception magic. It didn't render him invisible, but it did make people less likely to notice him. Made people who might feed information back to Carlisle less likely to see him and take note of the direction he was heading in.

It would have worked, too, as long as Carlisle himself wasn't the one to see him.

The man felt eyes on him. He repeated the magical mantra over and over, but the sensation would not go away.

The hairs on the back of the man's neck stood upright with alarm. His eyes darted back and forth until his gaze landed on a figure in the next carriage, staring at him through the window of the connecting door.

He saw a long, shadowed silhouette wearing a dark purple floor-length coat, ragged like an old shroud. A chalk-white face stared back at him with two black-circled eyes that burned like coals.

The man abandoned his mantra, his stomach turning, heart slamming against his chest.

As the train shuddered to a stop at South Kensington, the door between the carriages opened, and Carlisle stepped across.

Head down, the man bolted from the train, shoving aside complaining passengers that he neither saw nor heard. He didn't look back, he knew Carlisle had him pegged, and to even make eye-contact might be enough for his pursuer to bring him down.

He emerged on to the streets, his plan shot; a damp soap dancing from grasping hand to grasping hand.

'Hey, are you all right, mate?'

He didn't answer, didn't look to see who the concerned passerby might be. Instead, he ran and hoped a plan would come to him before he felt a cold hand grip his throat. He ran wildly and indiscriminately. Who knew, perhaps having no clear plan or destination would throw Carlisle off.

Why had he even told the Coven about Carlisle's illegal happy pill business? Why had he told Stella Familiar, who ran the place now since the death of her three witches? Because of his own short-sighted greed, that's why. He'd been the messenger boy for someone who disliked Carlisle muscling in on their turf. Not only muscling in but dealing in dodgy pills that were cutting down their clientele in ever-increasing numbers. Most of the gangs wanted to keep their customers alive, so when Carlisle started selling pills cut with who knows what—pills that had the unfortunate side effect of stealing years off a user's life—well, they took exception to that. It was bad for business.

Of course, they couldn't be seen to be dealing with the Coven themselves, so they offered him a fistful of cash instead, and the promise of more to come if he did the job right. But no one did the dirty on Carlisle and got away with it. He'd been stupid, and it was going to get him killed.

He ducked into a doorway to catch his breath, nervously glancing back to see how far ahead he was. Carlisle was nowhere to be seen. He felt a little hope twitch in his chest. Perhaps he'd been sharp enough to evade the great Carlisle. He'd always been fleet of foot when danger came a-knocking.

'Have you decided to stop? Oh good, running is so uncivilised.'

The voice was like velvet.

The man didn't turn to it, he just ran.

There!

There on the ground, a way out, an escape hatch to another place.

He pulled the metal manhole key from his pocket and fell to his knees, jamming it into the sewer cover, wrenching it up, and wriggling down into the dark to land with a wet thud several metres below. His eyes instantly became accustomed to the sudden switch from light to dark, glowing in the gloom, two large yellow beacons.

Even before the sewer cover fell back into place, he was away. His body begged him to stop, but the man knew he couldn't, not with death at his heels. And so he ran through the dark, his feet splashing through the damp trickle that snaked across the old stone floor of the sewer.

He knew the sewers well. He'd grown up down there, in the labyrinth network of tunnels that ran like veins under the skin of London. He knew every twist, every dark turn, every hiding place. He hadn't stepped out into the world above until he turned double figures. He felt better here. He was in his element in the sewer, and maybe—just maybe—it would give him the edge over the beast that stalked him.

It did not.

Something struck his ankles, twisting round and round and bringing him crashing to the slick, hard ground.

'No. No!'

His hands scrabbled at the rope that bound his legs together, but the rope only pulled tighter, like a python squeezing the life out of a dinner that had yet to accept its place on the menu.

'I'm sorry,' the man pleaded. 'I'm so sorry!'

'I don't care,' came the reply.

Carlisle drifted out of the shadows, the other end of the rope in his black-gloved hands, his heavy boots splashing through the water.

'You told tales on me, sewer-born. I find that extremely rude.'

'They made me!'

'Oh?'

'Yes, yes. I had no choice!'

'The way I heard it, you sold me down the river for money. Tacky.'

'It was a lot of money.'

Carlisle threw his head back and laughed, his shoulder-length black hair dancing as his howls echoed around the stone tunnel.

'I hope you had time to enjoy your bounty young man, because now I am going to snap your neck.'

With a flick of his wrist, the rope that bound the man's ankles detached and coiled back into his hand. He opened his coat—the inside rippling and glowing as though the lining were fashioned from stars—and fixed the coiled rope to his belt.

The man scrambled backwards, unable to rise, unable to escape.

'You should be proud,' said Carlisle, 'most don't make it as far as you did before they find my hands on them. You're a nippy little whippet.'

He flexed his slim fingers, his mouth a red slash across his pale face.

But the man still had one card up his sleeve. A rumour he'd heard that might yet save his life. 'I know where your artefact is,' he cried.

Carlisle stopped his advance, the corners of his mouth twitching down momentarily. 'And what do you know of my artefact?'

'I know three things,' the man replied, his back resting against the brick wall of the tunnel, heart beating almost to the point of giving out as he looked up at the figure looming over him.

'You have my curiosity, sewer-born. Please proceed.'

'I know you want it. I know you lost it.'

Carlisle raised an eyebrow.

'And… and I hear a rumour that it's been found.'

Carlisle reached into his pocket and pulled out a red apple. He polished it against the soft fabric of his purple coat, then took a bite. 'Temptation,' he said. 'Like the snake to Eve in the Garden of Eden, you sit there, tempting me with juicy, sweet information. But as you can see, I already have an apple of my own.'

'I don't… what?'

'What's to stop me beating the information out of you then killing you anyway?'

'Well… it's not good manners…?'

Carlisle chuckled and took another bite of his apple.

'So? Do we have an understanding?' asked the man, rising slowly, his hands flat to the wall. 'My life for the whereabouts of your missing artefact?'

Carlisle took another bite of his apple, then bowed his head once in agreement. 'Very well, you have my word. Tell me the location and I will not kill you.'

The man felt a little relief wash over him. 'It's in Blackpool.'

'Blackpool?'

'Blackpool,' he confirmed. 'It is understood that your artefact is in the possession of a great magician.'

'I see. And who fed you this juicy morsel?'

'An eaves, who heard it from an eaves, who heard it from an eaves.'

The man felt Carlisle's eyes boring into him, interrogating him.

'So? Are we good?' he asked.

'Good enough. Congratulations, you live to scurry amongst the rats another day.'

Carlisle tossed the apple into the air as he turned, caught it with his other hand, and walked away into the black.

The man held his breath, listening to Carlisle's footfalls as they drifted away and away until he couldn't hear him at all. His legs almost unhinged as the relief crashed over his body like an angry ocean wave against a crumbling cliff face.

He'd done it. He'd crossed Carlisle, been caught red-handed, and survived. He felt like laughing. Instead, he turned and ran in the opposite direction from where Carlisle had disappeared, feeling elated, until finally he could run no further and slowed to a stroll, heading for a sewer cover that he knew opened up outside his favourite pub, where he could drink long and hard to celebrate his good fortune.

As he stopped beneath it and pulled out his tool to lever the cover open, his foot nudged something on the ground.

The man looked down, expecting to see a stone, or the partially-rotted corpse of a sewer rat. What he actually saw made his eyes widen and his stomach drop.

It was a red, half-eaten apple.

He felt the hands around his neck just long enough to realise that his life was at an end, then his neck was snapped and he crumpled to the ground.

'One thing you should know about me,' Carlisle told the lifeless heap before him, 'I lie.'

He placed his foot against the man's head and pressed down until the skull cracked beneath the heel of his boot.

4

The office at Blackpool Central Police Station that Rita had worked out of for the last five years smelled like old pizza and fried chicken. Officers weren't meant to eat hot food at their desks, but with the amount of hours they spent there—not to mention nights—it was more or less a daily occurrence.

Rita flopped into her chair, her nose wrinkling at the familiar background scent. She leaned back to put her feet up on her desk and almost kicked a teetering tower of overdue paperwork on to the well-worn carpet. She looked up at the ceiling, which had once been white but had long ago taken on a yellow hue from decades of detectives hunched at their desks smoking. Not that they'd been able to smoke in there for years, but then the place was slow to spend money on touch-ups.

'What time d'you call this?' asked DI Collins, the question emerging from beneath a moustache several shades darker than his hair.

'Time your wife finally cleaned that shit out of her eyes

and left your fat arse,' replied Rita, to a chorus of approving laughter thrown in Collins' direction.

'We're literally two minutes late, Collins. Traffic,' said Waterson, 'by the way, I know it's you who blocked up the bogs last week.'

'You can't prove a thing.'

The whole office turned to eye Collins, who suddenly found his computer screen very fascinating.

'Hobbes, Waterson, in here,' said DCI Alexander Jenner, poking his balding blonde head out of his office into the main space, cutting any further arguments dead.

DCI Jenner closed the door to his private office behind them as Rita and Waterson entered and stood before his desk.

'What was that about?' asked Jenner, thumbing over his shoulder as he made his way around to his chair.

'Men's bog, Guv,' replied Waterson.

'Collins admitted to blocking it yet?'

'No, Guv,' said Rita.

'Third time in a month. Someone seriously needs to look at that man's diet.'

Rita smirked. As far as bosses went, DCI Jenner could be a lot worse. Oh, he yelled, he expected way too much of them, and was just downright unreasonable at times, but somehow he managed to pull off the trick of being likeable at the same time.

'Got something for us, Guv?' asked Rita.

'Woman. Jane Bowan. Her partner, boyfriend, says she's missing.'

'How long?' asked Waterson.

'It's been two days. Uniform have done the usual missing persons job, but family insist she hasn't just walked out. Here,' he tossed over a plastic folder containing all the information gathered so far. Rita snatched it up.

'No clothes missing, no bags or suitcases gone, her phone still on the bedside table, her bank account hasn't been accessed,' reported DCI Jenner. 'She just disappeared. So find her.'

An hour later, Waterson pulled to a stop across the road from the house Jane Bowan and her boyfriend, Greg Nicol, shared.

'Nice area, this,' noted Waterson.

'Yeah, for Blackpool. Let's keep things in perspective, Waters.'

'Water-*son*. Water-*son*. For my own sanity's sake, just try it out, please.'

Rita made a show of considering his plea, then frowned. 'Nah, sounds weird. Shall we?'

Waterson smiled and shook his head as they stepped out of the car and headed over to the blue door of the house.

Rita had been thinking about putting in for a transfer to London. To be truthful, she'd been thinking about it for the last four years, but this year, this was the year she was going to do it. She'd written up her transfer letter, printed it out, put it in an envelope, and sat it in the top drawer of her desk at the station.

Before the year was out.

She had to do it.

She'd been stuck in that small, shuffling town her whole life. It was time for something different. Something more. Her stomach ached at the idea of another year cooped up in that frayed little place, living on the edge of the world, if you could even call what she did living. She hadn't had the heart to mention her plans to Waterson yet. Sure, he heard her bad-mouth the place on a daily basis, but he had no idea she was actually about to go through with it, and kiss the town goodbye.

Rita was actually a little worried about how he'd take the

Hexed Detective

news. She and Waterson had been partners for years. Yes, they bickered, yes, they fought, but they were each other's rock. Best friends, really. She knew when she told him she was leaving him behind that he'd take it as a betrayal. He wouldn't say as much, he'd probably even wish her well, tell her congratulations on finally doing what she always said she would, but she knew, under all the blather, the sense of betrayal, of abandonment, would cut deep.

But Rita didn't have a choice. Blackpool was suffocating her. One more season spent in that small-minded, clapped-out town and she'd lose her mind. She needed to get out of there. To start over somewhere new.

A man answered the door, He looked like he'd had about a year's worth of rough nights, his eyes red and unfocused, his skin pale.

'Mr Greg Nicol?' said Waterson.

He blinked as if confused, then slowly nodded.

'I'm DS Hobbes,' said Rita, showing the man her badge. 'This is DS Waterson. Can we come in?'

'Yes, right, of course.'

He turned and they followed him through to the front room. Greg sat in a chair, then hopped back up, dithering. 'Sit,' he said, 'please, down.'

'Thank you,' said Rita, as she and Waterson sat on the couch.

'So, is there news? Good news?' asked Greg.

'Not yet, I'm sorry,' replied Waterson.

Greg ran his hands through his mess of dark hair. For a moment, he looked as though he was about to crumple to the floor in tears, then reined in his emotions, nodded, and sat back in the chair again.

'We've been put on your case, Mr Nicol,' said Rita.

Waterson folded his hands in his lap. 'We're here to ask you a few questions that should help us get a picture of this from your perspective. You'll have answered these questions a hundred times, I'm sure, but if you wouldn't mind going over your story one more time.'

'No, no, of course not. Happy to.'

Rita took out her pocket notepad and a pen, ready to scrawl down his answers in a handwriting that was legible only to herself. 'Can you take us through what happened?' she asked.

'Yes, of course. But like I said before, it's just… there's really not much to say. Practically nothing, it's all so bloody… so… I don't know what.'

Rita gave Greg Nicol her best, "I understand", face. All police had that down to a fine art. One year they'd even given out an award for it at the office Christmas party. Waterson won. Kept the little plastic trophy in his bathroom.

'Okay. Well. It was morning. I always get up before Jane, she likes to hit the snooze another couple of times, but I get up. Alarm goes off and I'm up. And, well, the thing is, that was the last time I saw her.'

'When you got out of bed?' asked Waterson.

Greg Nicol nodded.

'So you left for work and didn't see her again?' asked Rita.

'I heard her. Before I left, I mean. I heard her turn off the alarm and get up. Heard her moving around upstairs. I had a tonne of work at the office piling up, so I'd decided to get in early and get a good quiet hour in before everyone else turned up. So I shouted goodbye up the stairs and rushed out the door.'

Rita nodded and took it all down in her notepad. 'Did you hear from her again? Phone call? A text message? Anything at all?'

'No. I sent her a text at lunch. I always do. Just a little, "love you", text.'

Hexed Detective

'But she didn't reply?' asked Waterson.

'No. No, she didn't. That's not unusual—sometimes she leaves her phone turned off at work—so I didn't think anything of it.'

'I see,' said Rita. 'And how long was it before you realised Jane was missing?'

'About two hours after I got back from work, so just after eight. That's when I started to get worried. She wasn't answering my texts or calls, and then I found her phone in the bedroom. I called Kate, her friend—they work in the same office—and she said Jane… she said Jane hadn't turned up to work at all. And she hadn't called in to say she was sick or anything, either.' Greg Nicol bent over, head in his hands. 'Oh, Christ. She's dead, isn't she? Jane, she's dead. She's fucking dead.'

Rita stood and went over to the man, patting him on the shoulder. It was meant to be reassuring but came off more like she was petting a friend's pet dog that she didn't quite trust not to snap at her fingers.

'We don't know that, Greg,' she said. 'Let's assume not until we have reason to, okay?'

Greg looked up at her with red, bleary eyes. 'Can you find her?'

'We're going to do our best, Mr Nicol,' said Waterson.

'We were getting married,' said Greg. 'Been engaged almost two years.'

'When's the wedding set for?' asked Rita.

'It's in two weeks. *Was* in two weeks.'

Waterson gave Rita a look she recognised. He was thinking it was possible she'd ghosted him. Decided the marriage wasn't for her and cut out.

'Had she been acting strange at all?' asked Rita.

'Strange?'

'Just anything out of the ordinary,' she replied. 'Anything

you noticed in her actions, in the things she said. Anything different about her behaviour that stuck out to you?'

'No, nothing. She was excited about the wedding.' Greg Nicol said this, then his brow furrowed.

'What is it?' asked Rita.

'Well, she'd been having bad dreams more often recently. She told me that.'

'Since when?' asked Rita.

'Just in the weeks leading up to her... to her not being here anymore. But it was just a few nightmares, what could that have to do with anything?'

Rita and Waterson left Greg Nicol and Jane Bowan's house and headed for the car.

'So,' said Waterson, 'bride-to-be gets the jitters as the big day looms, gets stressed, starts having nightmares, then one morning she cuts out and holes up somewhere because she can't face telling her hubby-to-not-be that it's all over. That sound like a possibility to you?'

Waterson got behind the wheel as Rita looked back to the house, doubt itching at her.

'Yeah. Maybe.'

Razor liked London at night. It was the best time to skulk, and he prided himself on his skulking. He could spend hours surreptitiously moving his way from bar, to street, to library, to car park, his ears twitching at every conversation that came his way, searching for something useful. He knew by a person's body language, by their tone of voice, whether the information being shared was worth storing away for future use.

A little light rain began to spit, and Razor popped up the collar of his grimy leather coat, the bottom hem of which was tattered from where it met the ground. Razor was an eaves, and like all eaves, he looked a little like a person and a little like a mutated mole. His eyes were beady, his ears pointed, hair coarse and close-cropped. And just like the rest of his kind, his mouth was full of needle-sharp teeth that could bite clean through a finger with little effort.

His snub nose twitched at the centre of a face that had seen better days. More than one fist, more than one blade, and more than one set of brass knuckles had left their mark upon what had never been the most aesthetically pleasing of mugs.

Razor dealt in secrets. In information. In whispered words. All eaves did. This was their role in the Uncanny world. If something was worth knowing, chances were an eaves had heard about it, and would be willing to pass the information on, for a price.

And the price they named? Magic. Just a taste. It nourished an eaves, and it kept them safe, which was just as well, as trading in secrets was wont to put a target on your back. Their dens, which twenty or more eaves at a time would call home, needed to be secure, else someone with a grudge creep inside and slit their throats.

So, with each new secret that was passed on, an eaves would swallow a portion of magic for nourishment, then hold the rest back to add new twists, dead ends, and meandering passageways around their den. Only an eaves knew how to traverse the impossible tangle of doors and streets they created – doors and streets that had no business connecting to one another. Only an eaves could navigate such a labyrinth.

Razor opened a door which, for anyone else, would have led to the inside of a fish and chip shop, but when Razor stepped through, he found himself inside an abandoned warehouse almost a mile from where that chip shop stood.

He marched across the open space, the metal roof creaking in the wind, before stepping out into the men's bathroom at a prestigious Leicester Square cinema. Razor snatched up the box of popcorn that a man who was urinating had left perched by the sink, then entered the third stall. He didn't break his stride as he found himself not facing a toilet, but walking across the roof of the British Museum.

As Razor munched the popcorn and headed towards the metal fire escape, he felt prickles shoot up and down his squat, thick neck, and spun around, dropping the stolen popcorn, fists clenched, ready for a fight.

A tall man in a long dark purple coat was sat upon an incongruous comfy reclining chair, reading a book.

'Razor, I was wondering how long I'd have to wait for you to pass through.' Carlisle waved a book at him. 'A little over two hundred pages, as it turns out.' He stood and slipped the dog-eared paperback into an inside pocket of his coat.

'You got him then, did you?' asked Razor. 'The young sewer-born lad?'

'I briefly made his acquaintance, yes,' replied Carlisle, a large, easy grin spreading across his pallid face. 'In fact, if you'd like to say farewell to the poor soul, I do believe some of him is still attached to the bottom of my boot.' Carlisle lifted his foot and waggled it in Razor's direction. 'No? Suit yourself.'

'What d'you want, Carlisle?'

'Oh, what does anyone want in this life? To feel free and happy, with a belly full of food and a song in one's heart.'

Razor was ready to rush him, as pointless as he knew that course of action to be. But Razor was a fighter, and if it came to it, he could take a lot of punishment before his life was given a brutal full stop.

Hexed Detective

'Oh, Razor, please, stop it. I mean you no harm, I promise. You may unclench your everything.'

'I know what your promises are worth.'

Carlisle laughed and clapped his hands together. 'Point taken. But no, I'm not here for any fisticuffs, I'm here merely for the valuable service that you and your kind provide to the likes of mine.'

Razor shuffled as his brain tried to work out what Carlisle was on about.

'Information, my squat, muscular friend. Information.'

'Right. That I can do. And do I get a taste in return?'

'Now, now, you know that is beneath me, Razor. No taste, but you'll get to go home to your den without any new marks on that pummelled lump of meat and bone you call a head. How does that sound?'

Razor knew it was the best he could expect, and nodded, hissing through his small, sharp teeth. 'I let you know about the sewer boy's visit to the Coven, what else d'you want?'

'You did, and I am most grateful, believe me, but in his final attempt to cling to his woeful excuse for a life, he shared with me a sliver of information he thought I would be interested in.' Carlisle stepped forward, cupping Razor's head in his hands. 'And, oh dear, ugly thing that you are, it was information that fairly made me tingle from toe to nose.'

The silence crushed.

'I would've told you,' said Razor.

'Is that so?'

'Eventually, I would've. I just… I didn't know how legit the news was. Honest.'

'Now, let's not sully the moment with lies, Razor.' He released the eaves' head and moved past him, stepping up on to the edge of the roof and looking out over the city, the surrounding office lights shining through the dark like distant stars. 'Is what the late sewer-born said true? Has my artefact been spotted in Blackpool, of all places?'

'Yes, so they say.'

'They do say a lot, don't they? Any name for me to hold on to during my travels up north?'

Razor grimaced.

'A name, Razor.'

'Formby. The elder eaves in Blackpool. He's been heard to mention your... your artefact, when he's had too many ales. Says that someone in that place has it. Someone in Blackpool.'

Carlisle turned to him and grinned. 'Not for long, they don't.'

And without looking, he stepped off the roof and fell out of view.

5

Ellie Mason could have sworn it was the next right, then the next left, then on until the roundabout, but now here she was driving down a road she didn't recognise and the sky looked all wrong. It had a weird sepia tint to it, like a photograph in an old Western.

'Shit,' said Ellie. 'Shitty, shit, shit.'

Ellie had been to see a client two towns over and was now in a rush to get home to Blackpool. Her mum would already be throwing an epic fit. Ellie thought she had driven back the same way she'd travelled earlier, but now found herself driving up and down country lanes she didn't recognise, and of course, the sat-nav had decided to go on the fritz.

There were no signposts, no other cars in sight, so she decided the very best thing she could do would be to turn around and retrace her steps. Sixteen minutes later she realised with a heavy heart that she was as lost as she had ever been.

She pulled to a stop and checked her phone again, but found it still had a stubborn lack of signal. Ellie swore and struck the steering wheel with the heels of her hands. She was late. She'd promised her mum she'd be back home in time for dinner, and now she was late and getting later.

It was just then that she saw the house.

Ellie had not noticed the house until that moment, which seemed altogether impossible as it was so large, and situated directly in front of her. How had she not seen it? There were no other buildings along the road that she could see; indeed she didn't believe she'd passed so much as a garage or a bus stop since she'd wandered off the path somehow.

Ellie got out of her car and strode toward the front door. The house looked old. Very old. Vegetation covered much of the crumbling brick frontage, and several of the upstairs windows sported jagged cracks. If this had been a movie, it would be exactly the kind of house the main plucky heroine should definitely not approach, but always would.

'Probably abandoned,' Ellie told herself as she knock, knock, knocked on the front door, kicking up a tsunami of dust. She waited, but there was no response. Ellie gave it one last knock and then, just as she was about to turn and make her way back to her car, the door opened.

Before her, stood a man in a rabbit mask.

'Oh,' said Ellie, which was a reasonable response.

The mask encased the man's entire head and was topped off by two large ears that pointed to the sky like antennae. The mask was not plastic or rubber but covered with real, if tatty, fur. The man's outfit was no less peculiar. He wore an old suit of the sort that may have been fashionable when her great, great, grandfather was young.

'Hello,' said the man in the rabbit mask.

'Hello,' said Ellie.

'Do you like my mask?' asked the man as he stroked his large ears and smiled. Ellie did not know how she knew the man was smiling, but she did.

'It was my mother's, father's, mother's once upon a time when the mountains were small and the seas were song, or so the story goes. For a time it was lost to us, but I found it where I thought I would, in the forest, under a tree, and I dug, dug, dug it up.'

As the man spoke, Ellie felt a strange upside-down sensation in her stomach. She recognised that mask. She didn't remember her dreams most of the time, but this one dream—this one recurring nightmare that had poked and prodded at her for her entire life—this dream she remembered.

The dream of the rabbit mask.

'Now, Ellie, how may I help?' asked the man.

It was silly. Daft. Absurd. A coincidence of some sort, surely? Dreams didn't seep into the waking world.

'I wondered if... wait, how do you know my name?'

'Because you look like an Ellie.'

'I do?'

'Oh yes, and I look just how you'd expect a Mr. Cotton to look.'

Ellie looked back to her car and wondered why she wasn't already running towards it.

'Are you going to a fancy dress party?' she asked.

'At some stage, more than likely,' replied Mr. Cotton and his large ears twitched. Ellie ignored that because, of course, the ears were just part of a tatty old mask and so could not have twitched at all.

'I'm sorry to bother you, it's just I don't seem to know where I am, and my phone isn't getting a signal. Do you think you could direct me back to the main road? I'm sure I could find my way again from there.'

'You would like to be put on the correct path?' asked Mr. Cotton.

'I'm running late and haven't a clue where I've gotten to.

Daft of me, really. I don't know what happened, must have been daydreaming and taken a wrong turn or something.'

'So many wrong turns lurk where the right turn may be,' said Mr. Cotton, nodding. He clapped his white-gloved hands together and dust exploded, like a teacher slapping a chalk duster against the wall. 'I believe I would like to help, and I believe I will. My brother would also like to help.'

Ellie turned at the sound of someone breathing, rasping. Before her, stood a second man, shorter than the first, but dressed just as anachronistically. This one, the brother, wore a tatty hedgehog mask. As Ellie watched, spiders began to crawl out of the eyeholes of his hedgehog mask. Large, thick-legged spiders. Her breath caught in her throat.

'Don't worry,' said Mr. Cotton, 'my dear brother and I know exactly where you are going. Oh, we've known that for a long, long time.'

Ellie's mother called the police a little after nine that night.

6

Rita Hobbes and Dan Waterson were sitting in the plush, warm front room of the house Ellie Mason shared with her mum. There seemed to be a numbers war raging between the amount of brightly-coloured pillows the room contained, and the amount of pictures featuring Ellie. The pillows were winning by one, as far as Rita could tell.

'Sugar?' called Janice Mason, Ellie's mother, from the kitchen.

'Two in one, none in the other, please Mrs Mason,' replied Waterson.

Janice Mason entered holding a tray with three china cups on it. 'Here we go, three lovely cups of tea.'

'Thanks,' said Rita, as Janice placed the tray on the coffee table and retreated to a plump, bright yellow chair.

'So,' said Rita, 'Mrs Mason, you haven't heard from Ellie now in almost twenty-four hours, is that correct?'

'Yes,' she replied, her hands worrying at the hem of her cardigan. 'I know I waited too long. Too long to call you. But she always tells me not to fret so much. She's an adult, she says. But, you know, it's hard when you're a mum. Hard to give them space.'

In fact, she had only waited two hours after the time Ellie had said she would return home before calling the police.

Normally Rita and Waterson wouldn't be asked to look into a case like Ellie's. At least, not so soon. She'd barely been gone twenty-four hours, and she was an adult. It was too early to know for sure whether anything bad had happened. But, as it turned out, Ellie Mason was the same age as Jane Bowan. Two females of the same age, in the same town, go missing without warning. Just disappear off the face of the Earth without taking any of their belongings with them, and without using their phones, or their bank cards.

But those weren't the only common denominators.

No, it turned out that Ellie and Jane had known each other. Matter of fact, they'd been in the same class in school growing up. Both officers had decided to keep Jane Bowan's disappearance out of the conversation, though. No sense upsetting Mrs Mason unduly.

'Could she have gone to a boyfriend's, or girlfriend's, without telling you?' asked Waterson. 'Could it just be a case of crossed wires?'

'No. No, no. We had a special meal planned, she would never forget that. And even if she had, why wouldn't she pick up her phone? I've rung and I've rung...' Mrs Mason broke off, pulling a paper tissue out of the now half-empty box perched on the arm of the chair and dabbing her eyes.

'Sorry if any of our questions upset you,' said Rita, 'we know how you must be feeling, but we need to get as clear a picture as possible to help us find Ellie.'

Mrs Mason smiled and composed herself. 'Yes, sorry, just all a bit frightening. I'm just so worried that I'll never see her again. That something... that something very bad has happened to my baby.'

No one liked this part of the job—sitting with frantic or grieving family members, telling them bad news, pushing them to answer a barrage of questions with their heads in pieces—but Rita had got used to it. Or as used to it as she could. She made it a rule to stay detached from people like Mrs Mason, otherwise, the job would have driven her to a nervous breakdown years ago.

'Is there anything you can tell us about the days, or weeks, leading up to Ellie's disappearance, Mrs Mason?' asked Rita.

'Like what?'

'Anything, anything at all,' said Waterson.

'Okay, well, let me think on that.'

'A change in her habits,' said Rita, 'a change in her way of acting around you, or other people. Maybe she said something that seemed odd but you brushed it off.'

'I really can't think of much.'

'If anything comes to you, anything at all, let us know, okay?' said Rita.

'Yes, definitely, I'll wrack my old brain and try to… well…'

'Mrs Mason?' said Waterson.

'It's nothing. Daft.'

'Let us decide that,' replied Rita.

'It's just, well, my Ellie has always suffered with bad dreams, off and on.'

'Bad dreams?' said Rita, looking to Waterson.

'Yes. About a man in a creepy old rabbit mask. Probably from some old film she watched that she shouldn't have. It's just, in the last few weeks, she started mentioning how she'd been having the dream a lot more. Almost every day. But I mean, I'm not sure how that can help you at all.'

Rita nodded and wrote *Rabbit Mask Dream* into her notebook. 'Thank you, Mrs Mason.'

E llie Mason opened her eyes.
Her throat was very dry, she ached, and she could feel the cold of the stone she was laid out on. She tried to get up, but found her wrists and ankles were attached to the stone; handcuffed?

Ellie felt terror. Deep down terror that robbed her of the ability to talk, to scream, to beg.

There was movement to her side.

Ellie lifted her head to see a figure step out of the gloom. The figure wore dark red robes. A goat mask covered his head.

Ellie tried to talk, croaked, coughed, attempted to regain control of her breathing, then tried again.

'Please…' her voice came out a thin whisper.

The figure didn't reply.

It was then that Ellie noticed what he held in his right hand.

It was an axe.

A hand axe, a wooden handle, a rusted metal blade.

'Thank you,' said the man in the robes, his fingers flexing around the axe's handle. 'Thank you so very much.'

R ita rolled off Chris Farmer as he panted and attempted to catch his breath, and looked up at her bedroom ceiling.

'Well done, you,' she said. 'Gold star.'

'Yeah, thanks,' he replied.

Rita sat up and reached for the glass of water from the bedside table, taking a sip.

'So,' Chris began.

'So?' Rita replied.

'It's really getting late.'

'Yup. You'll probably want to be heading home, what with it being a school day and all.'

'Right. That's absolutely what I was going to say.'

Rita knew full well that it wasn't, but she was in no mood to soothe his feelings. She was happy with their arrangement, especially as she was planning to fly the coop pretty soon. It wasn't her fault if Chris was looking for more. She had the feeling she was going to have to cut this sex-relationship off soon. Cut it off at the knees. It wasn't her fault. She never intended for him to fall for her. She never wanted to break his heart, especially as she'd still have to work in the same building as him. Awkward.

Chris leaned over and kissed her. 'Okay, I'm off, you cold-hearted, sexy, loveless thing, you.'

'Aw, that's the nicest thing I've heard all day.'

Chris laughed as he pulled his clothes back on, gave the side of the bed he'd just vacated a last wistful look, then said his goodbyes.

As soon as Rita heard the front door close, she stood and threw on the ancient, oversized t-shirt she wore to bed. She climbed under the duvet and was about to turn off the bedside lamp, but a thought itched at her. It was something Mrs Mason said, about Ellie having nightmares. And Jane's fiancé, he'd talked about her having nightmares, too. Of course, it had to be a coincidence... but when you added in the fact that they were in the same class together, suddenly it didn't seem like such a stretch to add it to the case file. It was another connection after all, no matter how crazy it sounded.

She checked the glowing digits on her phone. It was almost ten. Too late to call, really, but then this was about the case. She hustled downstairs, found the number in the file, and dialled. Four rings, and then he answered.

'Greg? Is this Greg Nicol?'

'Hi, yes, I'm Greg, who is this?'

'Sorry to call you so late, Mr Nicol, this is DS Rita Hobbes.'

His voice wavered, obviously more worried he was about to hear bad news than good. 'Oh, hello, yes, hi, what is it? Is there news?'

'We have a number of promising lines of enquiry,' Rita lied.

'Oh.'

Greg obviously saw through that one.

'I just wanted to ask you a quick question. I think it might help.'

'Okay, what question?'

'You said Jane had been having bad dreams before she disappeared, right?'

'Yeah. She'd had them all her life, but she'd been having them a lot more recently. Well, not "them", "it", the one dream. It was always the same one.'

'Was it about a man in a rabbit mask?'

There was silence on the other end of the line.

'Mr Nicol? Greg? Hey, are you still there?'

'How did… yes. Yes, she called it the rabbit mask dream. How did you know that?'

7

There were a lot of strange stories in Blackpool, and Formby knew them all. He knew the true stories, he knew the pretend stories, and he knew the stories that were both at the same time. Perhaps he knew those ones best of all.

Formby was an eaves. An old eaves. Some said he'd lived as long as any eaves ever had, though his exact age was unknown. He'd lived too long and outlived too many for anyone to keep score. It gave him a certain celebrity in the Uncanny world, or perhaps notoriety was more accurate. Formby enjoyed it. Some people almost feared him. Said any eaves that had lived such an ungodly long time knew things, terrible things, that no living creature should ever know.

Well, there was some truth to that.

Formby held secrets that must never be told. Truths that should always be denied.

But back to the stories...

Yes, Formby knew them all. It was an eaves' purpose to gather any and every bit of information that passed their large pointed ears. It all funnelled in and was stored in their memories. Everything they wanted to remember, and everything they didn't want to remember, was in there, and Formby, like any eaves, was able to access it when needed.

He knew the story of the Screaming Witch: a magical protector who fell for a demon and lost her mind. For laying down with a beast, the witch had been cast out of her coven —an unheard of thing—and was cursed to suffer never-ending torment.

It was said, when the night was cold and dark, that if you listened closely, you could hear the cursed witch's cries weaved into the whistle of the wind. A normal person might miss the sound, as most were not attuned, but the witch's screams were why the dogs of Blackpool were known to act strangely during a storm. To cower and bark and hide. They could feel the pain, the fear, and they wanted no part of it.

If ever you took a walk on the beachfront alone after midnight and were *very* unlucky, you might even have seen the witch, staggering across the black sand, her face a mask of pain. Should you have the misfortune of crossing paths with the poor wretch, turn and head in the opposite direction, because if she were to lay a barely-there, icy finger on your skin, you would drop dead on the spot.

Formby knew that story well, and had met with the Screaming Witch on many nights. Sometimes she was able to talk, to share scraps of information, but mostly she just begged for her torment to end. But there wasn't anything Formby, or anyone else, could do to help her.

He knew the story of the Devil Tree, too.

In Carsters Park there was a giant, twisted oak, upon whose thick, gnarled limbs no vegetation ever grew, and no snowfall seemed to settle. Legend had it that a demon had been summoned in the park by a cabal of dark magicians, only for it to attempt to break free of their control. The dark magicians were forced to attack, to send the beast back to

Hell, but part of the demon had remained. It sank into the soil and became part of an acorn that lay buried there, ready to sprout into an oak.

Young children who visited the playground in Carsters Park and escaped their parents' eyes would wander to the enormous tree and say they could hear it talking. Several of those children, after they grew into adults, said they never stopped hearing that tree. That its voice whispered and teased at them their whole lives, telling them terrible things and putting awful ideas into their heads.

More than one suicide note had made mention of the Devil Tree.

Blackpool was full of such black stories: dead things, awful things, pulled in by the tide and left beached on the sand. Sometimes, Formby wondered if Blackpool Tower's tacky light show was a beacon that attracted malevolence, drawing it in like ungodly moths with ragged wings, making them weave and dance before its fevered light.

And perhaps that was true.

Formby thought so.

Because above all else, he knew the story of the Blackpool Angel.

Formby stepped off the path, the wind blowing in off the sea, vicious and tugging at his coarse, brown hair, as though it were trying to rip chunks of it from his head. His battered old boots sank a little into the sand as he watched the surf wash in, and then drag itself back out again, an endless waltz.

He wondered if everyone felt that sense of unease as they looked out at the water. How was it possible that anyone—Uncanny or not—failed to sense it? To have it itch at their flesh. To have it ball a fist in their stomach.

But still, they came and built sandcastles and splashed out into the sea, screaming and laughing as they met the water's chilly embrace. For most, it was just the ocean. They had no idea about the creature that had sat out there, imprisoned before people had even walked across the land now called England.

Had no idea an Angel stood beneath the waves. And not just any Angel. This was one of the original seven, hand-crafted by God Himself, to sit at His side. A creature of almost limitless power. A perfect, divine being.

But even the divine could succumb to temptation. Perfection could turn to boredom, after all. And so it was said that the Angel made a deal with the Devil. A deal for power, for independence, away from God's side. God, of course, discovered the Angel had turned dark and unleashed His wrath upon the Blackpool Angel. A battle waged that cracked the earth and shook the skies, until finally the Angel was brought low and chained beneath the sea, between life and death, never to rise again.

And there it waited, still.

Was it the Tower, or was the Angel the beacon that attracted all manner of evil to Blackpool?

Formby shivered.

Rita followed Waterson into DCI Jenner's office and shut the door behind them. Jenner ignored them for a few moments as he peered at his computer screen and prodded warily at the keyboard with two fingers like it was the first time he'd ever used the thing.

Finally, he sat back and looked at the pair.

'Well?' he asked, as though they'd been keeping him waiting.

'Right, Guv,' started Waterson, 'here's what we know so far: two women have gone missing.'

'Yep, know that,' he replied, picking up a packet of mints and fiddling with it.

'Both women were the same age,' said Rita.

'The same age?' repeated Jenner.

'Yes, Guv,' said Rita.

'Huh. Bit of a coincidence?'

'Maybe,' said Waterson. 'Could be, but with only two missing so far, it's not enough to call it a pattern.'

'Go on.'

Waterson stepped forward. 'Neither of the women have been heard from or seen since they went missing. Neither have used their mobile phones, or accessed their bank accounts. Also, both went to the same school, Old Lane Secondary, same year.'

'Well, that's not a big surprise, considering they were the same age,' said Jenner. 'Did they know each other? Were they friends?'

'We're going to look into that,' said Rita.

'Okay, good work, keep me updated, all right?'

'Right, Guv,' said Waterson.

As he headed for the door, Rita dithered.

'You coming?' asked Waterson, hand on the doorknob.

'There's just one other thing,' she said.

Waterson dropped his head and sighed. 'The dream thing?'

'Yeah, it's weird, okay?' said Rita.

'Yes, agreed,' said Waterson. 'But it's just dreams.'

'I'm sorry, what are you two babbling about?' asked Jenner.

'Both the missing women, Ellie and Jane, they were suffering from recurring nightmares.'

DCI Jenner's eyes slid from Rita, to Waterson, and back again. 'Nightmares?'

Rita felt her insides squirm. She knew how daft this

sounded, and wished her mouth would just shut the hell up already. 'We were told that they were both suffering from nightmares, and that the nightmares had increased in frequency shortly before each went missing.'

'Right. So? People have nightmares. I have one about a clown who might also be my mum. It happens.'

'Yeah, but the thing is, it's the *same* nightmare. Both women were having the exact same nightmare.'

Rita turned to Waterson for support but found none.

'Two women are missing, possibly murdered,' said DCI Jenner, 'less nonsense and more proper police work, please, DS Hobbes. Hm?'

'Yes, Guv. Sorry.'

Waterson opened the door for Rita as she turned on her heel and strode out of Jenner's office, her cheeks burning hot with a cocktail of anger and embarrassment.

Every part of the Uncanny Kingdom has a place like Big Pins, the bowling alley come drinking hole, two streets away from Blackpool's beachfront. Big Pins was a private place, hidden from the rest of the population, where Uncanny sorts could gather, talk, and drink, without having to hide who, or what, they were.

Big Pins, like all of these places, was secreted down a blind alley. Most passers-by would not notice the entrance to the alleyway – to them, it would appear nothing more than a continuation of the brick wall either side.

But Carlisle was not like most passers-by.

He strode towards the secret entrance to the blind alley, his coat flowing back in the wind like a cape, his boots clomping across the cobblestones.

Carlisle did not like Blackpool.

Hexed Detective

He had paid the place a visit just once before, perhaps seventy years ago now, and vowed never to return. He found it a tacky backwater. A grim excuse for a town, with little obvious charm or reason to stop itself toppling into the sea. His opinion upon arriving for the second time was in no danger of changing.

He walked down the cobbled street of the blind alley, his skin tingling as he felt the wash of concentrated magic rolling around him. The world swims in magic, but in some places, it is more concentrated than others. Here, in this alleyway, it made Carlisle's eyes dilate, and the corners of his usually downturned mouth twitch into a smile.

He stopped, looked up at the slowly-blinking neon sign that announced Big Pins existence, and sighed. He pushed his way inside, a fug of warm air and unfortunate smells rushing out to greet him. As he stepped across the threshold, Carlisle felt an energy slide by him like the parting of a beaded curtain. Big Pins was protected by a magic-dampening bubble, and with good reason. Uncanny sorts gathered there to drink night and day, so the dampener acted as a safeguard. A safeguard against a drunken fight getting out of hand within Big Pins' walls; a fight that might otherwise lead to undue damage and loss of life. You were meant to feel safe inside such a place, so the dampening bubble gave all who entered—all who drank and bowled and gossiped—a little peace of mind.

Carlisle stopped as the door swung closed behind him, and took the place in. He'd visited Big Pins during his last visit, and it looked as though it had been renovated since then. Possibly sometime in the mid-seventies judging by the awful decor, which was a worn 1970s version of a '50s U.S. bowling alley. It was every bit as tired and tacky as it sounded, but that, as far as Carlisle was concerned, was Blackpool all over.

He made his way to the bar, past the venue's six ten-pin bowling aisles, all of which were in use by semi-inebriated clumps of flotsam. As he passed through the place, Carlisle was pleased to note that certain clusters of people turned to shield their faces when they saw who had entered. It seemed his reputation preceded him. Carlisle smiled. He did enjoy engendering a sense of unease. A frightened man was a man on his back foot, and someone, potentially, to use.

Carlisle reached the sticky-topped wooden bar and took a stool. 'Barkeep, a pint of your least objectionable inebriation, please.'

A giant lunk of a man in a bowling shirt turned from polishing the optics and eyed the widely grinning Carlisle with small, hooded eyes set deep into a tombstone face. 'Huh. Back already?' asked Linton, the owner of Big Pins.

'And blessed do I feel to make your acquaintance once again, Linton my fine, fearsome fellow.'

Linton raised what was probably an eyebrow, but may have been a fistful of wire wool taped to his forehead, then grabbed a pint glass and began pouring a drink.

Carlisle turned as aisle four cheered a strike. 'I see you've decorated.'

'Yep,' replied Linton, plonking the pint down in front of Carlisle and spilling a good quarter of it in the process.

'Yes,' said Carlisle, 'I don't like it.' He picked up the glass and took a mouthful. 'Now, this on the other hand, this is a step up from whatever swill you were serving during my last visit.'

'I do not expect any trouble in my establishment, Carlisle,' said Linton, placing a scarred baseball bat on the counter.

Carlisle eyed the much-used object and recalled his last visit, when the thing had made contact with the back of his

Hexed Detective

head. 'You wound me with such suspicion, Linton, old friend.'

'I'm not your friend, Carlisle. I don't believe you have friends.'

'Well, they do say you can judge a man by his closest company, and I am fabulous company.' Carlisle offered up what would be best described as "a shit-eating grin" as Linton sighed and placed the bat back beneath the counter.

'So what is it then?' he asked. 'On your holidays?'

'Please, I do not holiday. Holidays are for the idle and simple-minded. No, no, no, I am here to speak to a gentleman whom I believe makes frequent patronage of your fine, sticky-floored rat hole.'

Linton crossed his thick arms across the broad barrel of his chest. 'He's not here.'

'You don't even know who it is I'm after.'

'Likes of you? You always want something. Information, most likely. And where do you best get information from but an eaves? And everyone knows which eaves you seek out first 'round here.'

'Linton, I do believe you've grown smarter in your old age. Did you go and read a book like I suggested the last time we met?'

'Drink your drink, leave, and I'll let Formby know you want a word with him.'

'So he's not here?'

'What did I say?'

'I see. Of course. My apologies.' Carlisle stood, finished his drink, and turned to leave. 'Just one thing,' he said, turning back to the bar and pointing off to a darkened, far corner of Big Pins. 'Who is that ugly old thing over there, trying to hide?'

Linton's eyes twitched to the figure shrouded in gloom, then reached down to grab his bat.

'It's okay, Linton,' said Formby, leaning forward to reveal his face. 'He can ask his questions if he pleases.'

'Formby,' said Carlisle, 'you are here after all! Well, would you look at that, Linton, you big mountain of a man. Formby, that wretched old eaves, is here after all. What a stroke of luck.'

Carlisle turned from the bar and strode over to join Formby, taking a stool opposite, his long coat reaching down to the worn carpet. 'I take it you knew of my imminent arrival.'

Formby nodded and smiled. 'Not much escapes these old ears, your majesty.'

Carlisle raised an eyebrow to that greeting, but let it pass. 'Razor spread the word, did he?'

'That's so, aye,' replied Formby. 'Can I get you a drink?'

'That's okay, I like the look of yours.' Carlisle reached forward and picked up the pint Formby was halfway through, raising it to his lips and slowly consuming the remainder before gasping, smacking his lips, and placing the now empty glass back before the eaves.

'Well,' said Formby, 'that was a bit of a dickish thing to do.'

Carlisle clapped his hands together and laughed. 'Has Razor also informed you of the reason for my return to this godforsaken shit hole?'

'Aye, he has at that.'

'And is what he says true?'

Formby shifted on his stool.

'You will tell me,' said Carlisle.

'It's true enough.'

Carlisle smiled wide, though to Formby it did not appear pleasant, more like a shark readying itself for lunch.

'Well then, where is my artefact?'

'A magician has it.'

Hexed Detective

'A magician? Ooh. And would this magical practitioner be known to me, old-timer?'

'Old-timer? I understand you are even older than I, Carlisle.'

'Ah, you are old, ancient in fact, but I am timeless.'

Formby snorted. 'I might use that in future if you don't mind.'

'So, this magician, who is it?'

'I don't know.'

The smile dropped from Carlisle's eyes. Perhaps the shark would feast after all. 'You would not be telling me porkies, now, would you?'

'I swear to it. I know the artefact was discovered, and I know that it is still here in Blackpool, in the hands of a magician. But neither I nor anyone I have spoken to seems to know who this magician fellow is. Believe me, I have tried to find out. He has not mixed with the rest of the Uncanny world, it seems. Kept himself to himself all his years.'

Formby swallowed as Carlisle's eyes bored into him, and very much hoped the gloom of this corner of Big Pins was adequately hiding how much he was sweating.

'A magician,' said Carlisle, finally stopping his visual interrogation.

Formby sagged back slightly in relief.

Carlisle stood and flipped a coin on the table in front of Formby. 'For the drink.'

'Thank you.'

'If you hear any whispers on the wind about this magician, you'll send them to my ears alone, I trust?'

'Of course,' said Formby. 'You have my word.'

'The word of an eaves? Well, now I can sleep soundly.'

'There's one other thing,' said Formby.

'Go on.'

'Women are going missing. Some say the magician is involved.'

There was another drunken cheer as a fresh set of pins was cleared with one bowl.

'Christ, I hate Blackpool,' said Carlisle, then pulled his coat closed, and headed for the exit.

8

The Old Dog was situated across the road from Blackpool Central Police Station, and as such, was always crammed with off-duty officers. It was a small, snug pub with an ancient TV set that was always tuned to one sports channel or another.

At that moment, as Rita was sat slumped and grumpy, nursing half a pint of lager and scowling at anyone daft enough to say hello, it was showing a snooker match. Rita closed her eyes and listened to the *click-clack* of coloured balls sliding across the baize.

'This seat taken?'

Rita looked up to see a beaming Chris Farmer, still in his uniform, already lowering himself on to the stool opposite her, drink in hand.

'Looks like it is now,' said Rita.

'Oh. Well, I can always...'

'No, it's fine, you're there now, so.'

'Right. You know you're a very tricky woman to be around.'

'Aw, you sweet talker.' Rita grinned and winked as she took a drink.

'So, there was something I wanted to talk to you about,' said Chris.

'I thought we'd settled this already. No sleeping over.'

'No, not that. You've made yourself really, really clear on that one. I mean, really, really, incredibly, brutally clear.'

'It's not that I don't like you,' replied Rita, flushing a little.

'Look, it's not about me and you, whatever me and you actually is. It's about the case you and Waterson are on.'

'Oh? What about it?'

'I overheard Waterson and Benton talking. About you.'

'I don't like the sound of that.'

'Waterson was talking about some rabbit mask dream thing.'

Rita sighed and sat back, sloshing the liquid in her glass around.

'Yeah, he thinks I'm being an idiot. But both missing women had the same nightmare. I mean, the exact same nightmare. How can that not mean something?' She knocked back a slug of beer. 'You think I'm mental, right?'

'No. Well, a bit, but not because of that.'

'Thanks.'

'It's just... this dream, right. It was about a man in, like, a tatty old rabbit mask, yeah?'

'Yeah, why?'

'My cousin, Gemma... have I mentioned Gemma?'

'You've mentioned Gemma.'

'She used to tell me about a bad dream she had growing up.'

Rita sat forward sharply and clenched her pint glass so hard it was a wonder the thing didn't shatter. 'She had the dream? Gemma had the rabbit mask dream?'

Hexed Detective

'Yeah. That's a bit weird, right?'

Three people? Three women, all having the same nightmare? Rita felt a knot in her stomach. She was right. There was something to that dream. Something important that was connecting these people. It might be irrational—it certainly wasn't something DCI Jenner was going to believe—but it wasn't nothing.

'Chris, where did Gemma go to school?'

'Old Lane Secondary. Why?'

They left their half-finished drinks on the table as Rita headed for the exit, dragging Chris behind her as Ronnie O'Sullivan settled down over the snooker table and attempted to pot a tricky green.

Greg Nicol opened his front door to see a strange specimen stood before him, grinning widely.

'Hello?' said Greg.

The strange man bowed slightly, then straightened up. He wore a long dark purple coat that had seen better days, and had skin as white as fresh-fallen snow.

'And you must be one Mr Gregory Nicol,' said the visitor, his voice honeyed and posh.

'That's right,' said Greg. 'Can I help you?'

'Yes, I understand that you can. May I be granted entrance to your charming home?'

Greg must have agreed and let the man in, because a few short minutes later he found himself handing the man a mug of tea, though he did not recall actually agreeing, nor the man entering his house. It was the strain of Jane going missing, that was it. The lack of sleep, the lack of resolution. That feeling of being in limbo. No word, no body, alive or dead, impossible to say; Schrodinger's Corpse.

'I'm sorry,' said Greg, sitting down in an armchair, 'I'm sure I've already asked you, and you've already told me, but I'm not really on the ball at the moment. Who are you?'

'My name is Carlisle, and I'm here about the missing woman.'

'Are you police? A detective?'

'If you like,' said Carlisle, and reached into an inside pocket of his coat. As he did so, Greg caught a glimpse of the lining and was sure he saw colours dancing, stars twinkling.

'Here,' said Carlisle, holding up a piece of card, 'my credentials.'

Greg peered at the card and felt a little queasy. There was one card, but there were also two cards, and Greg's poor stomach churned as his eyes strained. One of the cards appeared to be a yellowed-with-age, and of course now useless, Blockbuster Video membership card. The second card announced his visitor as Detective Inspector Carlisle.

'My credentials,' said the man again, his voice warm as it flowed into Greg's ears.

He blinked and the sick feeling vanished, as did the Blockbuster Video card. The man, Carlisle, held only one card, and it showed he was indeed a detective here about Jane.

'Is there any news?' Greg asked warily. Any visit or phone call from the police made him worry that this would be when the bad news finally arrived and triggered his complete mental collapse.

'I have no idea,' replied Carlisle, taking a sip of tea.

'Oh. Right. So why are you here?'

'As you said when you greeted me at the door; you can help me.'

Greg was confused by this, and again began to wonder about the Blockbuster Video card. Surely it had been that after all?

'What can you tell me about the disappearance of your partner?'

'I've already told you lot everything I know over and over, I'm not sure I have anything else I can add.'

Greg looked at the man's clothes again. The strange, ragged coat, the big, scuffed, heavy boots, and thought it was a very strange way for a detective to dress. Greg now noticed with some concern that the man appeared to be sniffing at the air like a dog. 'What's wrong?' he asked.

'Something has been here.'

The man placed his cup of tea on a sideboard and fell to his hands and knees, sniffing at the carpet.

'Could I look at your identification again?' Greg asked.

The man slapped the floor with one hand then leapt back to his feet and strode towards him, causing Greg to back up until the wall stopped him.

'Something has been here,' said the man again, looking down at him. Greg was a reasonable height, but the man, Carlisle, towered over him.

'I don't understand what you mean.'

'Neither do I. Not exactly. But I can smell it. Taste it. Something to do with… dreams.'

Greg blinked.

'Tell me about dreams, Greg.'

'Well, it's like I said to the other detective—'

'Other detective?'

'Yes, DS Hobbes. Jane has always had these bad dreams. These nightmares.'

'Yes, yes, yes, that's it! Not just dreams; nightmares.' The man turned on his heels and headed for the door. 'What was the nightmare about?'

'Jane said she used to see a man in an old rabbit mask.'

The strange perhaps-detective paused in the doorway and

glanced back, his brow knotted. 'I am very sorry for your loss.'

The words hung heavy in the air as the man left, and the front door opened and closed.

Greg felt the words slowly become part of him.

Felt the truth of them.

Loss.

He knew it was true.

Jane was never coming back.

Three hours later Greg was still curled up in a ball on the carpet.

Rita didn't like Gemma Wheeler's house. It was too neat, too orderly, too sparse. It was one of those homes that looked like nobody actually lived there at all.

'What's this about, Chris?' asked Gemma, who looked a lot like a chubbier version of Chris in a long, curly wig.

'This is Rita, my…' he looked to her for guidance.

'Colleague.'

'Right. Just my colleague and, sort of, acquaintance.'

'Okay. So…?'

'Gemma,' said Rita, 'have you heard about the two women who went missing recently?'

'Yeah. It's been on the local news and that, hasn't it? Terrible stuff. Makes you worry. Why?'

'Well,' said Chris, 'it's just Rita here's on that case, and I thought you might be able to help. Sort of.'

Gemma looked blankly at her cousin.

'Jane and Ellie; did you know them?' asked Rita.

'Yeah. Well, I didn't *know them* know them, if you get me. But they were in my year at school, so I knew who they were. We weren't friends or anything, though. Spoke a couple of times, maybe.'

'The couple of times you spoke, did the subject of dreams ever come up?'

There was that blank look again. 'Dreams?'

'Gemma, tell Rita what you told me about your nightmares. That thing you've dreamed about on and off since you were little.'

'Why?'

'Gemma,' said Rita, 'do you dream about a man in a rabbit mask?'

Gemma's face flushed and she took a step back. 'Why'd you tell her about that? That's private, Chris!'

'Jane and Ellie, they had that recurring nightmare, too,' said Rita, pressing on.

'What? That's... well, that's weird, isn't it?'

Rita and Chris both agreed that it was weird.

Gemma stepped back again. For a second Rita thought she might actually collapse, she'd gone so pale, but instead, she slowly lowered herself down on to the couch. 'I don't like that dream,' she said. 'The rabbit mask dream. I don't like it.'

'What happens in the dream, exactly?' asked Rita.

'Nothing. Not really. At least nothing I can remember. I just have this person in a rabbit mask, and I don't like the rabbit mask. It's old and mouldy, and I know it stinks, and I can hear his breath in there.'

Gemma was starting to clench her fists, over and over. Chris sat next to her, trying to calm her.

'I can hear his breath rasping against the inside of the rabbit mask and I'm really, really scared he's going to take the thing off and I'll see what's underneath, and I know if I see it I'm going to lose my mind. I feel like he wants me for something. Has always wanted me for something, and there's nothing I can do.'

'Okay, there, there, that's enough,' said Chris, as a tear began to roll down Gemma's cheek.

'How can the three of us have the same nightmare?'

'I don't know,' said Rita, wishing she had something soothing to tell the poor woman. 'The dream, the nightmare, have you had it more often recently?'

Gemma Wheeler nodded, and Rita began to feel very worried indeed.

Rita's phone informed her that it had just passed 2 a.m. and she wondered again just what the hell she was doing sat in her car staking out the home of Gemma Wheeler.

Chris had gone on shift, so for the last five hours, Rita had been alone in her car, waiting for... well, waiting for something. It was fair to say that they'd worried Gemma with their visit, and Rita felt a responsibility. To what? To stop anything bad happening to Gemma? She realised that in many ways, this was crazy. That she'd taken it upon herself to become a woman's bodyguard because she shared a nightmare with two missing persons.

She'd already ignored two calls from Waterson—who was no doubt wondering why his partner had gone M.I.A—but how could she explain what she was doing to him, or to anyone else? It was clear he thought she was bonkers for deciding that the dreams were a line of enquiry worth pursuing. She couldn't say she blamed him. It *was* bonkers, but it also felt so completely and utterly right.

She thought about Chris, about how he'd come to her with information about his cousin and the dream. He'd not questioned things, hadn't said anything about it being a mad coincidence, he'd just picked up the thread and handed it over. Rita couldn't help but feel a little grateful, not to mention impressed. Chris had a more open mind, clearly, than many others on the force.

Oh, God, thought Rita, *don't go getting real feelings for him.*

She didn't notice when her eyes grew heavy and started to droop, but at some point she realised she was no longer sat inside her car in the middle of the night but was now stepping on to Blackpool beach, looking out at the sea.

There's something in there.

Beneath the waves.

Something dark and terrible and ancient beyond words.

It was out there, the thing, desperate to break the surface and step on to the land again.

What was it?

It wasn't a person, it was definitely an *it*.

'We fought it,' said a glowing man with great wings attached to his back and a halo shining so brightly it hurt to look at. 'We fought for centuries, the sky burning with fire. And we won. We stopped the beast that it had become.'

Rita nodded like she understood. Maybe in the dream she did, for a moment.

Then she looked out to sea and saw something awful dragging itself out of the waves and rushing, screaming towards her.

Rita awoke with a start, reflexively pushing herself backwards before she realised where she was. She wasn't on the beach, she was in her car, and it was bloody freezing. It was now just past four in the morning, and Rita decided she'd had enough. She reached over to the car key and was about to turn it when she noticed the face staring in at her from the passenger seat window.

Only it wasn't a face, not as such. It was a mask. A tattered old rabbit mask.

'Shit!' Rita jumped back, but the figure was gone.

She looked around, out of every window, head jerking this way and that, but she couldn't see the rabbit-masked figure anywhere.

'What the fuck?' she said quietly, and began to worry he'd just ducked down out of view. That he was crouched low and out of sight, ready to scare her again, or worse, grab her.

Maybe it was just a remnant of the dream? Yeah, that could be it. She'd been having a weird dream, and when she was still just half-conscious, still caught in the dream's wake, she'd seen something that wasn't there.

But what if…?

She looked over to Gemma Wheeler's house.

The front door was wide open.

'Shit, shit, shit!'

Rita threw the car door open and half-jumped, half-fell out of it, racing towards the house, pulling out her standard-issue baton and flicking it to full extension.

'Gemma!'

She ran through the open door, sprinting from room to room, but she already knew. Somehow you can just tell when a house is empty. You feel it, hear it.

Rabbit Mask *had* been there.

And now Gemma was gone.

9

DCI Jenner sat low in his chair and rubbed his eyes. 'So, the man in the mask was there, and then he wasn't?'

'I know how it sounds,' replied Rita. 'I mean, it sounds mental. I sound like a mental person.'

'Agreed,' said Jenner, looking over to Waterson, who was stood mute by Rita's side. 'And did you see this incredible disappearing fancy dress man?'

'I wasn't there, sir.'

'I was following my instinct on my own, Guv,' said Rita.

Jenner sat back in his chair, and Rita could practically feel the weary annoyance emanating from him.

'With all due respect, a woman did go missing,' said Rita, steaming ahead, 'Gemma Wheeler. She told me she had the same dream as the first two women, and now she's gone.'

'We don't know that yet for sure,' Waterson cut in.

Rita turned to him and tried very, very hard not to punch him in the face. 'I saw the man in the rabbit mask. Her door was wide open, phone and money left behind.

Gemma gone, same as the others. On top of that, she's the same age; even knew the other two. Well, a little bit.'

Waterson raised his hands and eyebrows and took a step back. 'I agree, there's a pattern, but it's only been hours since she was last seen. That's not enough to write her up as a missing person.'

Rita may have said a swear word or two, then turned back to Jenner. 'Guv. They're linked. You must see that.'

Jenner sighed, then nodded. 'Yes. There's a link. An actual, solid link that you can follow. Same age. All women. All went to the same school. That's what you dig into, agreed?'

'Agreed,' said Waterson, making sure he was out of his partner's range.

Rita wanted to voice her complaint, but she could see she wasn't going to win that battle. Fine. If neither of these stupid men wanted to include the rabbit mask dream in the overall picture, then she'd include it on her own.

Clear of Jenner's office, Rita attempted to bore a hole through Waterson's head with her eyes.

'Hey, stop that,' said Waterson, swatting the imaginary laser beams aside.

'Thanks for the back-up, *partner*,' Rita spat.

'What do you want me to do? You're talking about dreams, Rita. We can't build a case on mask-wearing dream people. Dreams aren't taking these women, a person is.'

'Okay, it's weird, Waters, I get that, right, but it's *something*.'

Waterson dipped his head and sighed, then looked back up at her. 'Rita, I've followed you down some weird old paths, but I'm not gonna play the Scully to your Mulder this time. For one thing, I don't have the legs for a skirt.'

Rita glared at Waterson.

'Not gonna crack a smile at that, eh?'

She was not.

After the third furious round of drivers spanking their horns at her, Rita thought it best that she stopped driving angry, and pulled over until she'd calmed down.

She yanked the wheel over, parked up, and stomped towards the beach. Rita had never really cared for the beach. To her, it just highlighted the fact that she was on the edge of things. Away from anything interesting. Away from a better, new life.

Plus she'd had sex on the beach once and the sand had got everywhere. *Everywhere.* You don't forget that sort of chafing in a hurry.

She sat down heavily, dug her hands into the sand, and threw a great clump of it at the water. The wind caught it and threw it right back at her.

'Stupid, fucking wind!' she yelled before looking around to make sure no one had seen her picking a fight with the elements.

She wanted to be angry with Waterson. No, actually, she wanted to be completely bloody furious at him. The problem was, she could see where he was coming from. DCI Jenner, too. She knew they were right. What use was it chasing a nightmare? It's not like they could lock the thing up. And apart from asking every woman in Blackpool of a similar age to Gemma and the other missing women if they'd ever dreamt about a rabbit mask, it was useless as a means of finding other potential victims.

And here was the main point: it didn't help her find those who had already gone missing. It was a link, a really strange link, but it didn't help her get any closer to finding out what had happened to them, or where they were. Waterson was right. Not that she'd ever tell him that. But he was right. They had to work the other, tangible facts. Chasing phantoms wasn't going to save those women, or any others.

'DS Rita Hobbes, is that you?'

Rita jerked back at the sudden intrusion to see a tall, pallid man in a long, purple coat smiling down at her.

'Who's asking?' she replied, pushing herself up on to her feet and taking a step back to create a safer distance from the man, her hand ready to pull her extendable baton.

'We met at some police function or other, I think. Don't tell me you don't remember.'

Rita peered closer at the man and found herself caught by his wide, dark eyes. They seemed almost to shimmer. To draw her in. To make her not want to look away. 'Function?'

'Yes. Two years ago, perhaps? I'm DI Carlisle, do you remember me now?'

Rita shook her head, breaking eye contact. It felt like she'd taken four shots of vodka in quick succession. 'Two years?'

'That's right. We met and spoke, very briefly.'

Something seemed to tease at her memory. It was like she almost believed him. Almost. 'Can I see some ID?'

The man's smile grew somehow wider, revealing more teeth than seemed possible for one person's mouth. 'But of course. Where are my manners?' He reached into his coat and pulled out a card. 'There, look, DI Carlisle.'

Rita looked at the card, then back at the pale, tall man, and then back at the card again. 'I see,' she said.

The man nodded and pocketed the card.

The thing was, Rita really did see. And what she had just seen was not the identification of a detective in the police force, but a yellowed, useless Blockbuster Video card.

Was he trying some Jedi mind trick on her? Some Derren Brown-style mentalist magic? Or maybe he was just some random nutter. Well, whatever he was trying to do, it had completely failed. Not that Rita had to let the strange man know that – better to let him continue his ruse and find out just what his game was.

'Sorry, I think I do remember you now, actually. At that police function.'

'That's right.'

'Yeah, names and faces, not my area.'

'Well, that is unfortunate, considering your line of work.'

Rita laughed, or at least pretended to. 'So, what do you want, Inspector?' she asked.

'I understand you are in the midst of a most fascinating case.'

Rita's hand twitched towards the baton again. 'Yeah, it's an unusual one all right,' she replied.

'You see, I've been involved in a similar case down in London. Women going missing, men in animal masks—horrid situation—and I thought you and I could share everything we know so far, and perhaps assist each other. Now, doesn't that sound like a very good idea, Rita?'

She felt drawn to his eyes again.

'A very good idea,' continued the man, 'to tell me what you know.'

Rita wrenched her eyes away and staggered to one side, yanking out her baton. 'Okay, whatever it is you're doing, mate, you can stop, all right?'

The man raised an eyebrow and frowned. 'I'm simply trying to help out a fellow officer.'

'Really? I didn't know Blockbuster Video had its own branch of police.'

The man's eyes grew wide in surprise, then he laughed. 'Ah, you saw through my clever, clever ruse. I am impressed, Rita Hobbes. Most believe it with very little effort on my part.'

'Who are you and what do you know about the missing women? Are you involved?'

Rita began to slowly circle the man, a tactic she'd learned to keep the person off guard, off-balance, and keep oneself in control.

Unfortunately, the man didn't turn, didn't seem the least bit concerned. Instead, he stood stock-still and perfectly relaxed. He seemed more amused than anything.

'I'm just another concerned citizen, looking to bring an end to this tale of tragedy.'

'Right, of course, and if I were to search that coat of yours, I wouldn't find a rabbit mask stashed inside, right?'

'Oh, I'm afraid if I was that wicked fellow, and I was showing you my true face, you would no longer be standing, you would most likely have lost your mind completely.'

'I've seen him.'

The man turned now, curious. 'Oh?'

'The man in the rabbit mask. Just for a second.'

'Well. That's... unexpected. First the resistance to my charms, and now this. Aren't you full of surprises, Detective?'

'Who is he?'

'You do not wish to know.'

'Who is he?' Rita demanded.

It was stepping forward in anger, losing control, that did it. As the red mist descended, Rita had just enough time to see a flash of bright, shining teeth, before the man's fist connected with her jaw and things went very, very black.

10

Rita woke annoyed and confused, which was not an uncommon experience.

'Sucker-punching bastard,' she said, sitting up and rubbing her aching jaw.

She checked her phone. It didn't look like she'd been unconscious long; a minute or two at most. Rita got to her feet, still a little groggy, and slowly made her way off the beach and over to her car.

The case just seemed to be getting stranger.

She slumped behind the steering wheel and reached for a half-drunk bottle of water that had been sat in the car's passenger footwell for a good week. The water was tepid and a little foul, but it helped drag her the rest of the way back into the light.

Nightmares, people in animal masks that seemed to be able to disappear in an instant, and now this man. This strange, pale man with his odd way of talking, and eyes that made you want to believe things that were clearly untrue.

Carlisle, he said his name was. Rita wondered if that was just another lie. She'd have to use the name for now. She reached for her notebook and began to scribble down the events of her beach encounter. This man definitely belonged on the strange column of this case. The column neither her partner or her boss wanted anything to do with, but a column that was getting crowded and impossible to ignore.

It was just as she was about to start the car and drive home that something caught her eye in the rearview mirror.

It was a man, crossing the road, about fifty metres away.

The man's clothes looked very old-fashioned. Like something a gentleman might wear a hundred or more years ago. Oh, and he wore a rabbit mask.

Rita was almost knocked out for a second time as her skull connected with the window of the door in her rush to exit the car.

'Shit!' she said, rubbing her head as she stepped out, eyes searching for the rabbit-masked man.

She couldn't see him. Rita broke into a run, almost taking out a screaming cyclist as she did, as she sprinted in the direction it looked like Rabbit Mask had been heading in. Chip shops and souvenir stands stuffed with cheap tourist tat flashed by as she hurtled forward, skidding to a halt at the corner, and glancing wildly around for any sight of her quarry.

'You!' she shouted, grabbing the shoulders of a startled, elderly man. 'Police! Me! I am police! Have you seen a man? Man in a mask?'

'What? What man? What are you—?'

'Rabbit mask! He must have passed here, rabbit mask, rabbit mask!'

'What the bloody hell are yo—?'

Rita cast him aside and carried on running. How could she have lost him? It wasn't as if he could just blend into the crowd, not with those clothes and the giant, bunny ears—

There!

Hexed Detective

Wait, it wasn't him, this one was different. He was dressed the same, and had a mask on, too, but this one looked like a... like a hedgehog?

Rita shrugged and ran in the masked man's direction as he headed inside a games arcade. She stood, panting, a few feet into the garish, busy, and monstrously loud building. It was all claw games that you never won, penny-shove machines, and ancient shoot 'em ups. None of the so-called thrills on offer had changed since she was a kid.

Rita strode in, dodging the small, whooping children that scuttled by, almost bringing her down to the mangy carpet as she tried to squint past all the flashing lights and catch a glimpse of spines or rabbit ears.

A glimpse, that was all, of old, tatty fur, between the hustle and bustle, and Rita was off again, swerving through the public as though she were skiing a slalom.

'Oi, you! Stop, police!'

She found herself outside a set of double doors with the words PRIVATE stencilled on them, and didn't pause for a moment before pushing her way inside.

The dim room beyond was stacked high with dusty, broken games machines and large plastic bags full of soft toys, no doubt ready to replenish one of the machines in the arcade should anyone actually ever manage to win one.

Rita slowly pulled out her standard-issue extendable baton and edged further into the room, cushioning the door with one hand as it swung closed, masking the noise. She needn't have bothered. It quickly became apparent that she was alone.

'That's not possible...'

She began to search the room, looking for another way out—a window, a door, a fire exit—but there was nothing. There was only one way out, and that was the way she came in. Rabbit Mask had come through here though, she was certain of it.

'Shit, shit, shit.'

Rita sagged and leaned against the wall. It took a few moments to realise cool air was pooling around her ankles. Cool air that was emerging from the crack beneath the door she was leaning upon. A door that she was very, very sure had not been there moments ago.

Well, of course. Men in animal masks that come and go, and doors that appear by magic, Rita said to herself.

She stepped forward and placed her ear against the door, which looked like it belonged to an ancient, crumbling village church, and not the back room of a clapped-out seaside arcade.

Rita took a breath, then tried pulling on the door's cold, brass handle. It swung open and the cold from behind it wrapped its arms around her. Shivering, her breath now a fog, Rita flexed her fingers around the baton and stepped past the door and into what lay beyond.

What lay there was a dank, stone corridor, the arched roof of which was a little too low for her to stand up straight. Slowly, she made her way towards the light at the other end, her boots squelching across damp, mossy ground.

'Okay, okay, nothing to be terrified about, all perfectly normal…'

She glanced back to make sure the door she'd entered through hadn't disappeared, and was relieved to see the piled-up bags of soft toys still visible in the distance.

There were no other doors or windows in the corridor, just the opening ahead. A creepy stone corridor leading to a mysterious chamber.

Rita began to wonder if getting sucker-punched had done her some serious brain damage.

The corridor came to an end and she found herself before

the arched entrance to the chamber, the shadows of flickering flames licking across the ground towards her.

'Well, here goes something...'

Rita stepped into the room.

Rita wasn't sure what, exactly, she was expecting to find in the hidden room at the end of the stone corridor, but what her eyes took in as she shuffled into the chamber was certainly not it. It was Gemma Wheeler, Chris Farmer's missing cousin, draped in a blood-red robe, chained to a large block of stone.

'Holy shit.'

Rita raced across to the woman, who was a little too motionless for her liking.

'Gemma? Gemma!'

Rita slapped the woman's cheek, eventually rousing a groan. The woman's eyes flickered. She was still alive!

'Oh, thank bloody Christ,' said Rita. 'It's okay, Gemma, it's me. It's DS Rita Hobbes, your cousin's, uh, friend. I'm getting you out.'

That turned out to be easier said than done. The chains were heavy, locked, and fixed firmly to the block of stone she was laid out on. Rita had seen enough *Hammer Horror* films growing up to know what this sort of situation was leading to: a blood sacrifice. But this was twenty-first century Blackpool for God's sake, not some backwards village in the middle-ages.

'Help... please,' begged Gemma, her words a slur.

'It's okay, Gemma, I'm here. Nothing's gonna happen to you, okay?'

All well and good saying that, but she couldn't see how she was going to free the woman, not without leaving her alone and going for help. It was then that Rita noticed the stone altar, and what was perched atop it.

An axe. A small, old, hand axe.

Rita snatched it up. 'Looks like you're going to be doing more saving than killing,' she told it, and made ready to bash the chains, free Gemma, and get the hell out of there.

But as she turned, she saw that she and Gemma were no longer alone.

'Shit!' she said, jerking back in shock.

Stood in the entrance of the stone tunnel was a tall man in crimson robes. He wore a large goat mask over his head.

'Game's up, you sick bastard! Take off that bloody mask, right now!' The man didn't move. 'Look, you're done, I'm police, all right? And this is the last woman you or your other mask-wearing sickos snatch, you got that? Now kneel down and put your hands behind your head or—'

Rita wasn't sure what happened exactly, but there had been a flash of intense light, and what felt like a car driving directly into her chest. She sat up from where she'd been knocked down to see the robed man walking slowly towards her. Rita was in a horror movie, that's all there was to it, and this idiot was about to make her his latest victim.

'Not bloody likely,' she said, and grabbed the hand axe from where she'd dropped it, pushing herself back up and brandishing it. 'That's right, prick, you're nicked!'

As she ran at the man, he raised his hands and seemed to mould a ball of crackling, bright white light, his fingers dancing as though he were playing the air like a piano. Rita pulled to a stop and gawped. 'What is that? Stop that!'

The man did not stop. Instead, he raised the crackling ball of energy and threw it at her. She should have leapt out of the way, but—acting on reflex—she swung the axe at the ball. Rather than sending her flying again, the ball ricocheted off the axe and flew back at the masked man, hitting him and causing him to disappear in a puff of smoke.

Rita breathed heavily, staring incredulously at the spot

the man had been only heartbeats before. She stared down at the axe in her hand, then back at the vacant space.

'Holy crap.'

'Help…'

Rita shook off the shock and ran back to Gemma. 'Okay, hold still,' she said.

She lifted the axe high, then swung it down at the chain clasped to Gemma's ankle. To her delight and surprise, not only did the strike cause the chain to break, but all of the chains attached to her shattered and swung free.

'Huh, talk about lucky. Come on, you...'

Rita levered the still mostly out-of-it Gemma Wheeler up on her feet and guided her towards the stone corridor. As she went, she cast one final glance to where the goat-masked kidnapper had been standing before the ball he conjured bounced back at him.

'Yep,' she muttered, 'that beach bastard definitely gave me brain damage.'

11

Struggling under Gemma Wheeler's weight, Rita carefully weaved her through the games arcade and out onto the street, where she gently lowered her on a nearby park bench.

'Gonna… gonna kill… me…' Gemma panted.

'It's okay, you're fine, he's not gonna touch you, love,' replied Rita, sliding the hand axe into her belt and reaching into her coat for her phone to call for an ambulance.

'Emergency services, which service do you require, ambulance, fire, or police?' came the reply.

'This is DS Rita Hobbes, I require an ambulance,' she replied.

There was a silent pause.

'Emergency services, which service do you require, ambulance, fire, or police?' repeated the woman at the other end.

'Ambulance, I need an ambulance down at Archer's Old Arcade!'

Another pause.

'Hello? Can you hear me? What's the nature of your emergency?'

Hexed Detective

'Forget it!'

Rita hung up and shoved her phone back in her pocket. Blackpool's mobile phone coverage had always been spotty. Yet another reason to give the place the old heave-ho.

'Right, come on you. Let's get you to the hospital.'

Rita pulled Gemma back up to her feet and steered her down the street and back to where she abandoned her car. If Rita hadn't been in such a hurry, if she hadn't been more concerned with talking to Gemma, with keeping her awake, she might have noticed all the funny looks she was getting. The gawping stares from other drivers and their passengers as they sat together at traffic lights, or as she swerved by them at way past the speed limit.

But she did not notice.

Soon enough, the tyres of Rita's car screeched as she screamed to a halt in a vacant ambulance bay directly in front of the hospital's main entrance. She ran around the car, opened the passenger door, and attempted to get Gemma out and back on her feet.

'Gemma, come on, stay awake. Stay with me, love.'

It was no use. It had been hard enough moving her around when she was only half with it, now she was practically unconscious, and the dead weight was too much.

'Help! Give us some help here!' Rita screamed at a man as he approached, bunch of flowers in hand, exiting through the hospital's automatic doors.

The man didn't even glance at her.

'Bastard!' Rita spun back to Gemma. 'One second, I'll be right back.'

She ran into the hospital. 'Hey, I need help, I've got an unconscious woman in my car.'

The doctors and nurses gathered in the reception area ignored her.

'Oi!' Rita pulled out her I.D. 'Police. DS Rita Hobbes, I need help with a...'

Rita stopped. No one paid her the slightest bit of attention. In fact, a few of the nurses who had been huddled around a chart, turned and walked away.

'What is wrong with you idiots?' Rita cried.

She spied an empty wheelchair and grabbed it, pushing it through the automatic doors and back to her car. Through brute force, and a bit of colourful language, she managed to haul Gemma into the wheelchair.

'Right, you're okay Gemma. Here we go.'

She wheeled her into the hospital's reception.

'Oh my God,' said the large, female receptionist upon seeing Gemma, slumped in the wheelchair.

'Nurse Baxter, I need help!'

The receptionist and Nurse Baxter rushed over to Gemma; the nurse taking a knee, opening one of Gemma's eyes, and shining a pen torch into it.

'Hello, can you hear me? Can you hear me?' asked the nurse.

'Well, at bloody last,' said Rita. 'You're a bit oblivious in here, aren't you?'

'Who brought her in?' asked the nurse.

'What do you mean?' asked Rita.

'I didn't see anyone,' replied the receptionist. 'I looked up and she was just there.'

'Hello?' said Rita, waving her arms around. 'Have you two gone completely mental? I brought her in.'

'I think she's okay, but we'd better get her through and do some checks,' said Nurse Baxter, continuing to ignore Rita, who watched with confused astonishment as the receptionist grabbed the wheelchair and began to follow the nurse out of the waiting area.

'What, in the fuck, was that?' asked Rita, shaking her

head as she pulled out her phone again and dialled Waterson's mobile.

'Hello?' said Waterson, picking up on the third ring.

'Waterson! I found her, I found Gemma Wheeler! She's alive, I've got her over at the hospital and there's some really weird shit going—'

'Hello? Can you hear me?'

Rita swore, shook her phone, and stomped outside, hoping the reception would pick up better.

'Waterson, it's Rita, can you hear me now?'

'Sorry, I can't hear you, I think we've got a bad connection.'

The line cut off.

Rita looked down at her phone, then back over her shoulder into the reception area.

She was beginning to get a really bad feeling.

Carlisle stood in the stockroom of Archer's Old Arcade, looking through the doorway into the stone corridor beyond. He ran a chalk-white finger along the stone surrounding the ancient wood of the door, then sniffed his fingertip.

'Impressive,' he said, and stepped into the stone corridor beyond.

This kind of magic was beyond your common, lowly spell-slinger. They'd managed to sandwich two different places, in two different times, right next to each other. Carlisle couldn't even see the join. An eaves could do something similar, but not with different times, too. This was far beyond the ability of those wretched creatures.

Carlisle made his way down the old stone corridor, stooping low to prevent his head connecting with the arched ceiling. As he walked, he projected an aura of calm assurance, but inside he could not deny that he was concerned. He had hoped whoever had his property was some low-level fool—that retrieving it would be like taking candy from a baby—but this corridor told him that his quest would not be so simple.

Why did things always have to be so complicated?

He paused at the chamber's entrance and poked the toe of a boot at the chalk drawn on the flagstones in front of him.

It was a hex.

A booby-trap triggered by an unwanted visitor.

The trigger for the hex was a chalk circle with all kinds of arcane symbols expertly drawn within. Carlisle crouched and peered at each symbol, each rune, each magical oath. If someone had walked over this, it should have killed them. Should have turned them to ash in an instant. The hairs on the back of Carlisle's neck told him that the hex had most certainly been triggered, but he saw no evidence of ash. No little pile of dusty grey to indicate the trespasser's final resting place.

The hex hadn't worked.

Or at least, not in the way it was intended to work.

'Curiouser and curiouser...'

Carlisle stood and stepped over the now useless hex, not that such a trap would have worked on him, anyway. He had so many protections and totems sewn into the lining of his coat that it would take a magician of Giles L'Merrier's heft to fashion a hex that would even cause him a tickle.

The chamber was stone, circular, with a small altar stood a few yards from a large block of stone. A place of sacrifice then. A sacrifice disturbed?

Carlisle sniffed at the air. Magic had been deployed

within the space, and recently. A battle of some sort? Short, swift, over in moments?

There was dried blood on the large, central stone. The sacrificial stone. More than one person's blood. He thought about the man he'd visited; what was his name again? It didn't matter. The one he waited for was clearly long since dead. Murdered in the name of something.

Carlisle wondered just what that something could be.

But that wasn't why he was here. This was none of his business. He'd sacrificed more than one animal, more than one person, in his many, many years of life. Who was he to judge?

No.

His property, that's all he craved. It had been here. It had been used. He could feel it. Someone had removed it.

Something that didn't belong caught his eye, and he strode to one side of the chamber, crouching to pick up an item that had been left behind during the intrusion.

It was a black, standard-issue extendable police baton.

Carlisle lifted the baton and sniffed it.

'DS Rita Hobbes, I presume,' he said with a smile.

The Magician did not know where he was.

The world around him was indistinct shapes and colours and noises that he couldn't understand.

He tried to pull off the goat mask that encased his head, only to find he had no hands with which to achieve the task, nor a head to remove the mask from.

'Help me,' he pleaded. Or thought, or felt, or something else altogether.

How had this happened?

Where had he been?

The chamber!

She'd been in there. How had she found the entrance? No one should be able to find that door, that corridor. But even if she had…

…had…

had…

…

His thoughts drifted apart like blown smoke. Was that all he was now? A scatter of thoughts? Smoke on the wind?

How had she survived the hex?

He screamed, but how do you scream without a throat, a mouth, a tongue, an anything?

His own magic had been launched back in his direction.

Impossible and impossible and impossible, and…

The axe.

The tool of sacrifice.

She had it!

He was just a young boy, digging in the sand when his plastic trowel had…

Taken it.

Hidden it.

'I am here,' said the Angel.

'I failed,' the Magician replied.

'We cannot fail,' replied the Angel, its voice light and high, yet deep also, which was impossible and yet true and it filled the Magician to the brim. 'Can you see it?' the Angel asked.

'See what? Everything is chaos and nothing…'

'Can you see it?'

The Magician did see it.

The beach.

Blackpool beach.

And suddenly he was not nothing, he had arms to move, legs and feet to kick, and he was swimming, the seawater splashing cold against his face, the beach inching ever closer.

'I am here for you,' said the Angel, and finally the Magician crawled out of the sea.

The sand gripped between his fingers as he fell forward, the heavy seawater soaking the crimson robes that clung to his body. 'Alive,' he said.

The Angel had pulled him back from wherever his own magic had thrown him.

Limbs trembling, the Magician slowly stood and gulped great gasps of crisp sea air. 'Thank you,' he said, through blue, cracked lips.

'The work will continue,' said the Angel. 'Must continue. So close now.'

The Magician nodded. 'She'll have taken her to the hospital. I can go in after dark, some simple perception magic to hide myself. Steal into her room, kill her.'

'No. The axe. You must use the axe, you know this.'

'Yes. Yes, the axe.'

'Find the woman, reclaim the axe, complete the sacrifice.'

The Magician nodded as he took off his robes and folded them over one arm. This was just a momentary setback. The world would continue to spin. For now.

Rita had gone mad, that was the only explanation for it.

This time, as she drove towards the police station, she was very aware of the looks that were thrown in her direction. The shocked faces, the wide-eyed children tapping their dads on the shoulder.

For the thousandth time, she looked at herself in the rearview mirror.

There she was: wide green eyes, red hair. She was there. She was there.

It was that knock-out punch, it must have been. Things had gone all weird ever since then. Brain damage of some sort; temporary, hopefully. That could be the only explanation, because the other answer was impossible, and Rita Hobbes might be open to a little weird, but she did not mess with the impossible.

She screeched to a halt and burst into the station, rushing over to the duty sergeant at the reception desk.

'Arthurs. Arthurs, it's me. Can you see me?'

Arthurs was stood with a polystyrene cup of tea in one hand and a newspaper in the other, perusing the football results.

'Arthurs!'

She gave him a shove and Arthurs swore as the hot tea spilled over his fingers.

'Bastard!' he said. 'Bastard, bastard hot.'

Another officer, Matthews, looked up and sniggered. 'Daft git,' she said.

'This is… this is…' *Impossible*, was the word Rita did not want to say.

He hadn't seen her. Hadn't heard her. Even when she physically shoved him, he hadn't realised, hadn't noticed what had happened.

Rita turned and headed further into the station, passing people she saw every day. Not one of them acknowledged her. Not a "Hello", not an "All right, Rita?", not even a nod of the head. On any other day, not having to run a gauntlet of pointless greetings would have put a spring in Rita's step, but right then it felt like she was wading through treacle.

She made it up the stairs to the open-plan office she worked out of.

'Hey, I saved Gemma Wheeler,' she said. 'Found her, she

was gonna be murdered, but I saved her. Rita Hobbes, super cop.'

She wandered over to the desk of DI Collins, the toilet blocker. He was exploring the grimy insides of his left ear with the blunt end of a pen, periodically pulling it out and sniffing the end.

'Oi, Collins, we all know it's you that makes a mess of the bogs, you know?'

DI Collins raised his eyebrows in an appreciative manner at his latest pen sniff, then slid the poor thing back into his ear canal.

'Hello. Hello!'

She swiped at Collins' hand, sending the pen flying across the room.

'Shit it,' mumbled Collins, before selecting a fresh pen from his desk and continuing his disgusting excavation.

Rita sighed and walked to her desk, slumping in her chair as Waterson entered and sat behind his own desk.

'Hey there, Waters, it's me, your best buddy and partner, fancy indicating that I exist at all? You'd really be doing me a favour.'

Waterson opened the drawer of a filing cabinet and started sifting papers, ignoring her.

'Be like that, then. See if I care.'

Rita started as something clattered on the floor at her feet. It was a police baton.

'Feeling sorry for yourself, Detective?'

Rita stood up sharply and turned to the voice addressing her. She saw Carlisle sat cross-legged atop a vacant desk, eyes fixed on her, sipping a cup full of vending machine coffee.

'You!'

'Correct. What a sharp deductive mind you possess, Rita Hobbes.'

'You can see me?'

'Another hit! The mean streets of Blackpool are in safe hands.'

Rita looked around at the rest of the office, all ignoring her, ignoring him, just carrying on with their day-to-day work, oblivious. She reached down and grabbed the baton, brandishing it angrily at Carlisle.

'Please, Detective, I give you back your property and you threaten me? What kind of a thank you is that?'

'What is going on? Suddenly no one here can see me, or hear me. What did you do? Did you drug me? On the beach? Is that it?'

Carlisle raised an eyebrow and smiled a horrible smile. 'I'm rather afraid that, as far as the dreadfully ordinary world is concerned, you no longer exist.' He raised a second cup, 'Coffee?'

12

There was a small boy.

He was on his knees on Blackpool beach, blue plastic spade in hand, wearing only shorts as the summer sun beat down, warming his skin.

This was the Magician.

Would be the Magician.

But for now, he was just a boy, digging a hole in the sand.

It felt good to dig, to concentrate on something physical. To dig and dig and dig and think only of the hole. Of deepening it. Widening it. To no end other than the pleasure of the work. To no end other than to stop himself thinking about the bad things.

The boy felt sweat prickle on his brow as his slender arms continued to power the spade. She was crying louder now but he didn't have time to pay attention to that. Couldn't pay attention. If he stopped to comfort his mother then the hole would never get dug. So she whimpered and sniffled and pulled out tissue after tissue and the boy kept his eyes off her and on the hole in the sand.

He blamed her. He shouldn't blame her, he knew that,

but then who else was there to blame? She used to shout at his dad. Call him names. Make fun of him. Even at his age, he knew it was wrong to do that in front of him, but they'd argue anyway as he tried to concentrate on the TV.

He shouldn't blame her.

It wasn't her fault.

He realised he'd stopped digging. He looked up at his mum, sat on a towel with her legs folded beneath her, staring out to sea with red, raw eyes as if the answer to everything laid out there in the deep.

'Are you okay, honey?' she asked, without looking away from the waves.

He didn't answer. Instead, he went back to the task at hand. The hole. The ignoring her.

But it wasn't working anymore.

He dug harder, faster, but his cheeks were wet and his vision blurry.

Why did his dad have to go and kill himself? Why would he do something like that? Something so sinful? Bobby at school said it meant he'd have gone to Hell. Sinners went to Hell and there was no bigger sin than suicide, that's what Bobby's dad had told him. Bobby's still-alive dad.

His hands gripped the small shovel so hard it hurt. Hurt good.

His mum was crying louder now. He wished she'd stop. Wish she'd just shut up.

He dug, and his stomach hurt more and more as his anger grew, and he suddenly realised exactly who was to blame. Who he should be angry with. It wasn't his mum, or even his dad, who'd prepared the noose and placed his head through the thing.

It was God.

God should save. God should protect. His dad had been a God-fearing man. He went to church every Sunday without fail. He read passages from the Bible aloud every day before his evening meal. And yet despair had gripped him so tightly that it had caused him to resort to the ultimate sin.

Where had God been?

Did all the praying, all the years of being good and holy and right count for nothing?

Did anything mean anything to God at all, or was his dad just an ant? Were they all just ants? Ants that God would one day burn away with a magnifying glass, just for His own amusement?

God had abandoned his dad when he needed Him most.

God had killed his dad.

The shovel hit something solid and the boy was pulled out of his thoughts. What had he uncovered? Treasure? Probably just a rock.

He scraped away the rest of the compacted sand. What he found was not treasure, nor was it a rock.

It was an axe.

It wasn't a big axe like you might see someone on TV using to chop a tree down with. No, it was small, small enough for even a boy like him to use. He smiled and reached down, wrapping his fingers around the axe's wooden handle.

'I hear you.'

The voice made the boy lunge back and set his heart jumping. He looked around, but there was no one else on the beach. Just him and his mum, and it hadn't been his mum's voice. Besides, she was still too busy crying to herself, not paying him any attention at all.

He shuffled forward towards the axe, then reached out, hand trembling, and picked it up.

'I hear you,' said the voice, again.

The voice was faint, he could hardly hear it at all, but it was real. 'Who are you?' he asked.

'I am your friend.'

'Why can't I see you?'

'Because I must hide from something terrible.'

'From who?'

'From the most evil thing imaginable. From God.'

The boy had taken the small axe from the hole he had dug and hidden it in his bag. When his mum finally stopped crying and decided it was time to go home, the axe had gone with them.

The axe and the voice.

Years passed, and the voice grew stronger. He couldn't always hear it. Sometimes, at first, he'd go weeks without hearing a word. He'd go down to the beach, down to the exact spot where he dug the hole, and ask the voice to speak to him again. To keep him company. To make him feel less alone. But the voice would say nothing. Then he'd be drifting off to sleep, and there it would be, tickling at his ear.

'I am here.'

He would sit up in the dark, a smile as big as Christmas, and wrap his arms around himself.

As the years marched on, the voice grew louder still. Less like a whisper, more like a friend was sat right by his side, speaking to him clearly.

The voice became more constant, too. No more days or weeks of silence, the voice could always be counted on. If the boy wanted to talk, the voice would reply, and the boy would feel the warmth spread over him.

But the voice was not just a friend. The voice was a teacher. It told him he was right about God. God was not benevolent. God did not care about the creatures that crawled over this planet. God was petty and cruel, and the idea of a small boy's father taking his own life in a room where he knew the man's son would find him dangling like an abandoned marionette, filled God with glee.

Hexed Detective

'He laughs at us, at you. He laughs at your father,' said the voice. And the voice would know because the voice was that of an Angel. An Angel that had tried to teach God the error of His ways, and had been cast out because of it.

'We are brothers in pain,' said the Angel, and the boy pulled his covers close to his chin, his face a scowl, mouth a tooth-clenched grimace. And he nodded.

Yes, the voice, the Angel, was a teacher.

It did not just tell him about the evil of God's ways, it opened up a hidden world to the boy. A world of delight. A world of colour. A world of magic.

It started small—simple card tricks that anyone could do—but soon enough, the boy found himself able to do things he could not explain. The Angel told him the secret words, the secret shapes. Showed him the energy that washed all around him, around everyone, that most never saw. Could never understand, even if they did. Great multi-coloured washes, like the whole world was sitting at the bottom of an ocean. But instead of salt water, they swam through magic.

Swam through the Uncanny.

If you could see the magic—if you could learn to command it using the right words, the right shapes—then anything might be possible.

It did not always go right. Not at first. There was the time he tried to cheer up his mum, still broken five years after her husband killed himself. He put on a little top hat he'd made from cardboard and placed a box on the kitchen table. He told his mum he was going to make Nelson, their cat, disappear and then reappear.

He placed Nelson inside the box and put the lid on top. He waved his hands over the box and said the words he'd been taught. Felt the magic in the room begin to move towards him as though it were metal and he was now the most powerful magnet ever.

It soaked into him. Into his skin, his muscles, his bones. He said the right words, over and over, and then he opened the box.

Nelson was gone.

His mum had gasped, genuine surprise, genuine wonder. 'Oh my… how'd you do that, then? You're a little Houdini!'

The boy had smiled and laughed and his cheeks had flushed. He'd made her happy. Unfortunately, he hadn't been able to make Nelson reappear. He tried and he tried. He'd forced the magic into himself and said the words for hours and hours, until it felt as though he might sweat blood, but every time he opened the box, it was empty.

His mum had got cross then. Couldn't understand why he was playing up so badly. Told him to get Nelson back or he'd be grounded, and no supper, and slapped legs. He tried to tell her he didn't know where things went to when he disappeared them, but she told him to stop being silly.

The boy found Nelson the cat a few days later, washed up on Blackpool beach, dead. The boy fell to his knees and cried. Cried the tears he held back when his dad had died. Great, heaving sobs that shook his entire body. Tears that fell and soaked the very dead Nelson.

He didn't blame God.

Blame was too small a word.

Too insignificant.

'He doesn't care about you,' said the voice in his ear. 'He laughs at you.'

Yes, blame was too flimsy a word.

The boy did not blame God.

The boy *hated* God.

Hated Him with a white-hot fury that dried up his tears in an instant and threatened to turn his teeth to dust as he clenched his jaw so tight.

'I have a plan,' said the voice. The Angel of Blackpool.

'Will it hurt Him?' asked the boy.

'Oh yes.'

'Good.'

The boy carried Nelson away from the waves that threatened to reclaim him. Took him over by the groyne, the low barrier built to stop erosion, and began to dig the cat's final resting place.

'The evil He has done in the name of good,' said the Angel of Blackpool. 'The evil to you, to me, to Nelson. To everyone. He must be stopped.'

The boy nodded as he refilled the hole and hid the cat from his eyes.

'The axe. Sacrifice. We will grow strong. The axe will grow strong. Strong enough to free me. Strong enough to crack open the doors of Heaven itself.'

'And what then?'

'And then we will kill God.'

The boy stood and smiled for the first time since he'd seen his dad's purple face.

13

Rita ran out of the police station's reception and into the street beyond, hoping the cool outside air would whip some sense into her.

It didn't.

'This is mad. This is mad, this is,' she said, bending slightly, hands on her thighs, taking great gulps.

'Oh, this isn't even close to mad, I assure you,' replied Carlisle, gliding into the street. 'Why, I once visited a town where the laws of physics no longer applied. A great magician had gone mad with heartbreak and sought to take vengeance upon anything. Upon everything. Up was down. Cold was hot. Rocks had feelings that were easily hurt. All because a very plain woman refused his hand in marriage. Pathetic, really. Still, a knife to the neck put an end to that foolishness.'

'I'm sorry,' said Rita, standing, 'can you just stop saying words, 'cause none of the mental things you're saying are helping me feel any better. Like, at all.'

Carlisle smiled.

Hexed Detective

'Would you like to know what has happened to you, Detective?'

'That'd be nice.'

'I'm rather afraid, my flame-haired justice seeker, that you have been hexed.'

Rita frowned and nodded. 'Right. Hexed. As in, you know, magic and that?'

'As you say, magic. *And that*.'

Rita began to laugh. 'You're off your rocker, mate.'

'I do hope so, the entirely sane are entirely boring.'

'You're serious? A hex? A *hex*-hex. As in a hex? A magical hex?'

'Please stop saying hex, the word is losing all meaning.'

'But that's... that's stories, and stuff. There's no such bloody thing as magic. There's chip shops, and there's dogs, and there's disappointing men. Actual real things that you can see and touch.'

'Then how do you explain all of this? Excuse me,' said Carlisle, stopping a woman who was passing by. 'What do you make of my young lady friend's haircut?'

The woman looked to where Carlisle pointed, his finger inches from Rita's head.

'She believes it flatters her face shape, whereas I say it drowns her delicate features. What say you, madam?'

The woman began to edge away. 'What are you talking about, you nutter? There's no one there.' The woman hurried away as Rita rather self-consciously fussed at her hair.

'Okay. Point made,' she said.

'You found the stone corridor in the arcade. Found the chamber.'

'Yes.'

'You should not have been able to do that. Not someone so... ordinary.'

'Well, aren't you the charmer?'

'Then again, you shouldn't have been able to tell I was lying when I presented you with a glamoured I.D. And yet you did. Curiouser and curiouser do you become, Detective Hobbes.'

Carlisle began to slowly circle Rita, sniffing at her every now and again.

'Um. Rude,' said Rita.

'You do the impossible, and then you double-down and don't die when you're supposed to.'

'Sorry about that. I'm always doing what I'm told I shouldn't.'

'The hex was a booby-trap, to prevent the unwanted stumbling into the magician's place of sacrifice. It would have reduced much higher beings than you to dust if they so much as put a foot upon it.'

'Well, it didn't. It did whatever this is, instead. People can't see me, or hear me. I can touch them, but it's like they don't even register it. I'm some sort of... like a ghost, but not.'

'It is as though you... short-circuited the hex in some way. Which for someone as insignificant as you are is, of course, impossible. And yet...'

'And yet what?'

'Well, I am not currently conversing with a small pile of ash.'

'Fair point.'

Carlisle paused in his slow circling and clapped his hands together. 'Detective, I believe I must now lick your face.'

'Come again?'

'For purely scientific purposes, you understand.'

'Yeah, that's a hard pass, but thanks.'

'It's the only way for me to ascertain just what the hex has done to you, and if it is possible to reverse it.'

Rita shuffled, then grunted. 'Look, fine, but if I feel like you're enjoying it for even a second, you're getting a knee to your soft bits. Got it?'

'Consider it got.'

Rita shuddered as Carlisle gripped her face between his strong, icy hands, then bowed and licked her cheek.

'Well?' she asked as he straightened up and let go of her head. Carlisle rolled his tongue around his mouth with a look of disgust.

'Firstly, whatever face cream you are using in a vain and pointless attempt to halt the ageing process, tastes horrendous.'

'It's forty quid a tube. What else?'

'The hex fought. It could not do what it was created for, but a good hex does not give in. The magic wriggled and strained and it did the best it could for its master, to prevent you from hiding. From looking for help.'

'That's why no one can see me? Or hear me?'

'Anyone ordinary, at least.'

'To stop me getting in his way by getting help?'

'And that is not all.'

'Great, what else?'

'Something beyond awful.'

'Oh, God.'

'I would most likely walk into the sea and drown myself rather than suffer this second thing.'

'What? What is it? I'm dying, aren't I? Is that it? Am I dying?'

'Worse. I'm afraid… you are confined to Blackpool. You can never leave this stain upon the British Isles. I am so sorry.'

Rita had to try very hard not to make good on her earlier threat to connect her knee with Carlisle's genitals.

Being the sort of person who liked to see evidence before believing something wholeheartedly, Rita got in her car and went looking for proof of Carlisle's claim. Carlisle folded into the passenger seat, his head pressed against the car roof. Rita fired up the engine and drove to the outskirts of Blackpool.

'You know,' said Carlisle, 'your vehicle could really do with a clean. I believe these seats have stains upon their stains.'

Rita ignored him. 'Let's say I believe that magic is real and a magician is murdering women in Blackpool.'

Carlisle opened the car's glove box and grimaced at the landslide of crap that spilled out. 'Good Lord, woman.'

Rita went on. 'Whoever was doing it—the magician in the goat mask and the fancy robes—he's dead.'

'Oh?'

'Yeah. Well, I think so. He chucked some magicky rubbish at me, but I twatted it back at him and he disappeared. So he's dead, right?'

'No. I can... feel his presence still. It's like a sour taste at the back of my throat. He lives. He will return. His work is not yet done.'

'Right, great, fantastic. Aha,' said Rita, pointing at the sign they were about to pass that read YOU ARE NOW LEAVING BLACKPOOL.

'Brace yourself,' said Carlisle.

'For wh—'

Rita's response was cut short as the car slammed to a halt as though she had driven at speed into a brick wall. She was pretty sure she heard Carlisle giggling as she snapped forward and her forehead connected with the steering wheel.

'You're okay,' said Carlisle as Rita looked at him woozily.

'Bastard... airbag didn't work.'

'Again, supreme detective work, Miss Hobbes.'

Rita stepped out of the car, expecting to see the front end crumpled. Instead, her car looked fine.

'That's... what?'

Carlisle joined her, smiling. 'You did not crash into anything, the car was simply prevented from moving any further.'

Rita raised her arms and began to edge forward, as though moving through an unfamiliar room in the dark. As she reached the point the front of the car had stopped, she found she was unable to move any further. She could not feel a barrier, it was just suddenly impossible to go forward.

'Okay. Trapped in Blackpool. Crap.'

'Crap, indeed. I've visited some piles of unmitigated refuse in my many years, but Blackpool is a whole new level of horrid.'

All Rita had thought about for years was making the big move to London. Running from the town she'd spent her youth, shuffled from orphanage to foster care and back again. A pile of paperwork, not a person. She'd ached to finally leave the place behind and start afresh, but she'd left it too late and now she was trapped. Literally.

Rita screamed the word, "Fuck", very loudly until she ran out of breath and slumped down on to the side of the road.

'Eloquence and beauty,' said Carlisle, pulling an apple from his pocket and taking a bite. 'What a catch you are.'

'Okay, you seem to know a fair bit about me, so who the shit are you when you're at home?'

Carlisle smiled and swallowed, then tossed the half-eaten apple into the air, spun once, pulled open a pocket on his long, dark purple coat, and watched as the apple landed within.

'Allow me to make a proper introduction: my name is

Carlisle: thief, liar, charlatan, murderer, and once and future King of Great Britain.'

Carlisle bowed deeply, then rose again, a grin no one would ever trust stretched across his angular, pale face.

'Bullshit.'

'Bull-true.'

'King?'

'Once and future.'

'Then why aren't you in any of the history books and that?'

'There is history, and then there is *history*. We Uncanny sorts do our best to keep off the radar of you—how to put this kindly—you human garbage.'

'I feel like there was a kinder way of saying that.'

Carlisle chuckled.

'So why are you here? To stop the murders?'

'Oh no. What business is another man's murders to me?'

'Then what's with the interest in my case?'

'I have come to reclaim my property. An item that was stolen from me a long, long time ago.'

'What property?'

Carlisle smiled. 'An axe.'

Rita stood, her hand moving instinctively to the small hand axe that was tucked away in her belt, under her coat.

'That's the one,' said Carlisle, slowly approaching her.

'It's evidence.'

'It is mine.'

'It's been used to murder innocent women,' said Rita, backing up but finding she could move no further as she hit the Blackpool boundary.

'Murder innocent women? Are any of us truly innocent, Detective?'

'I don't care what mad shit is going on, I'm still a detective working a case, and this is the murder weapon.'

Carlisle stopped and nodded.

'Why d'you want it, anyway? I can point you to three different hardware shops where you can buy a brand new one. This one isn't even sharp.'

'It is mine. I will have it.'

'Why? Why's it so important to you?'

Carlisle paused, then looked Rita in the eyes. 'I will use it to reclaim my right. My throne. My crown.'

'Okay. How?'

'The axe is of Heaven. It provides certain… gifts.'

'Heaven?'

Carlisle nodded.

'Okay. Magic, magicians, Heaven. Fine. What kind of gifts?'

'The gift is unique to each person who wields it.'

Rita began to edge away from the impassable boundary and circle around Carlisle. 'I'm not going to give it to you. I told you, it's evidence.'

'Well, that is unfortunate.'

'Are you going to try and take it from me, because I will do you a lot of damage, scarecrow. Believe me.'

'Oh, I do believe you,' he replied, but Rita didn't think her threat had caused him any concern at all.

'Alas, I cannot just take it from you, which is… irksome.'

'Why not?'

'The axe can only be passed on if the wielder gives their true consent.'

'Then you're shit out of luck, Casper the Skinny Ghost. Women are being murdered in Blackpool. The fancy dress man responsible used this axe to kill them, and I'm going to bring him down. Until that happens, the chopper stays with me. Got it?'

Carlisle frowned, retrieved the apple from his pocket, took a bite, then nodded. 'A pact will be made, then,' he said.

'You what, mate?'

'I, Carlisle, true King of Great Britain, cruelly deposed, will help you stop this murderous magician who stalks the streets of your cesspool of a town.'

'And you'll get rid of this shitty hex on me, too, right?'

'Of course. When the magician is found, I will stop him, kill him, and the hex will be lifted.'

'Kill him?'

'It is the only way to end the hex.'

Rita wasn't sure how she felt about that. She was about justice, not murder, but maybe there was no other choice. She shook her head. They'd have to deal with that once they got to it.

'Okay, you help me stop this murderer, help me get back to normal, and I'll let you have the axe, deal?' Rita spat into her palm and offered it for a shake.

Carlisle looked at the hand as though she'd just proffered a fresh pile of horse dung. 'Please consider it shook,' said Carlisle.

'Germaphobe?'

'Sane.'

'Fair enough. So then, what's first?'

Carlisle climbed back into the car and Rita followed.

'First? Why, first we must visit the Night Fair.'

14

Rita was trying to play it cool. More to the point, she was trying not to entirely freak out in front of the insane, scary man who resembled an emaciated Richard E. Grant auditioning for a new Tim Burton film. The one who had, only a few hours earlier, left her knocked out cold.

They were driving towards Blackpool Pleasure Beach, a large fairground, popular with tourists, pickpockets, and teenage boys looking to cop a feel of something soft on the ghost train.

'Why did you call it the night fair?' Rita asked.

'You'll see,' Carlisle replied.

'Or you could just, I dunno, go ahead and tell me?'

'You'll see.'

'Right, be a cock then.'

Carlisle smiled, or at least exposed his teeth. 'Always.'

So she'd been hexed. It happens. Not to real people in really-real life, but it happens.

Well, no, it doesn't, but it had happened, and Rita was now as certain as she could be that all of it was real. She wasn't mad, or brain-damaged, and she wasn't going to wake up in bed and sigh in relief because it was all a dream. Probably.

Unless…

Rita pinched her leg and jolted at the sudden pain.

'Afraid not,' said Carlisle.

Definitely not a dream. What she wouldn't have given for a nice, hacky reveal right about then. Magic spells, magicians, murder? It was all a bit much, but it didn't change the fact that she had a job to do. A murderer to stop. She'd just have to go with it for now, at least until she knew for sure that the killer had been stopped. It was only then that she'd allow herself to fully freak out, curl up in a ball, and gibber incoherently.

But not now.

For now, she was still a detective, and women were at risk.

Rita pulled to a stop and she and Carlisle got out. She saw a sign pointing them in the direction of the Pleasure Beach. They'd have to go on foot from here.

'Come along, Hobbes,' said Carlisle, and strode off ahead, Rita having to almost, but not quite, break into a run to keep up with his long-legged strides.

'Oi! Little slower would be nice.'

He moved like a predator, like a shark cutting through the water knowing it had nothing to fear. Knowing that *it* was the thing to fear.

Rita placed her hand on the bulge of the axe, still tucked into her belt, hidden by her coat. A thing of Heaven? She wondered how much she should trust Carlisle. She touched her still tender jaw and knew the answer to that. He didn't care about the case, about women dying, he just cared about taking back what was his. For now, he was something she needed. He knew this weird world she'd fallen into, but she wouldn't let her guard down, because sooner or later, he was going to turn on her.

You never trust a wild animal.

You got an instinct for this sort of thing after spending that long on the force. People like Carlisle only looked after number one, and they didn't give a shit how many people got hurt because of that.

'I've got a question,' said Rita.

'Yes, your hair actually does compliment your face shape.'

'No. I mean, thanks, but not that.'

'Why did the axe bond with you if the magician did not give permission for it to do so?'

'Wait, can you read minds, too? If so, what am I thinking right now? I'll give you a clue: it's green.'

Carlisle sighed and shook his head. 'You are a prattling fool, Detective.'

'It was a bush. A bush.'

'It's a fairly obvious question.'

'And is there a fairly obvious answer?'

'No. I do not know why the axe agreed to become yours. It is... vexing. Not knowing is one of my least favourite pastimes.'

'Oi,' said Rita, as Carlisle veered away from the entrance to the Pleasure Beach, swarming as it was with tired-looking parents and sugared-up kids. 'That's the way in, the massive obvious entrance over there. There's even a sign that says "entrance" right next to it.'

'That's not where we're going,' replied Carlisle, not slowing.

'I thought we were going to the fair,' she replied, veering around a small boy with a face coated in candy floss and the wild eyes of a hopped-up junkie.

'Correct, but I do not believe I said anything about *that* fair.'

'Well, that's the only fair in Blackpool, and it's the one you had me park up in front of, so…'

'I said we were going to the Night Fair. The Night Fair shares the same space as your Pleasure Beach, but is not the same as your Pleasure Beach, understand?'

'Yep.' Rita stopped and thought about it some more. 'Actually, no. Not even a little bit.'

'You do surprise me. Just follow my lead.'

Rita was not a fan of being a follower, but follow she did.

'Wait,' she said, standing at Carlisle's shoulder as he stopped, 'that's not supposed to be there.'

'Isn't it? How peculiar.' Carlisle walked towards the large gothic metal archway in the side of a wall – a large gothic metal archway that really, really shouldn't have been there. The metal was coated in rust, and the arch stretched from one fire-blazing torch to another. The flames did not burn yellow-orange, they burned blue and green and made Rita feel funny.

'I know this place inside and out—unfortunately—and that entrance doesn't exist.'

'Not for you, not yesterday, not even a few short hours ago, but now your eyes have been opened,' said Carlisle. 'Welcome to the Night Fair.'

Rita remained still for a moment or two as Carlisle strode under the archway and into the strange fair beyond. A strange fair that appeared to be much gloomier than the late afternoon sun should allow.

'It's dark in there. How can it be dark in there?'

'*Night* Fair, Detective. The clue is in the name. Come along.'

Rita looked back to the Pleasure Beach's entrance, where someone queasy from the rides was throwing up noisily into a bin, then to the twisted metal arch in front of her, beyond which lay the Night Fair.

'Right. Good. Got it.' Rita shook her head and ran to catch up with Carlisle.

It was indeed gloomier inside the confines of the Night Fair. Rita squinted up at the sky to see stars twinkling and a full moon hanging heavy. 'We're not due a full moon for weeks,' she noted.

'It's always a full moon at the Night Fair,' Carlisle replied.

'It's also night here. How is it night?'

'Am I going to have to explain everything in triplicate? Keep close, it's easy to get lost in a place like this, and things that get lost are often never found.'

'I didn't realise you cared so much.'

'Of course, I care. If I lose you, I lose my axe. Now keep up.'

Rita kept up.

As they walked, Rita felt as though her head was spinning. This was nothing like the garish Pleasure Beach, this was older. You could taste the age, smell it even. There were no rides that she could see, but hundreds of stalls and tents crushed together as far as the eye could see.

In one stall, a large, fleshy man was waving in customers, taunting them, telling them there was no way any of them could toss one of his brass rings over one of the many trinkets laid out on a table, and for only a fiver a pop. Why anyone would want to win the prizes on offer puzzled Rita, as each of them looked as though they'd been fished out of a canal.

At another stall, what appeared to be a woman—but may well have been a large pile of rags that had swallowed a woman whole—was stirring a rusted pot of something that smelled so delicious it made Rita's stomach growl.

'Come on, then, Miss! Fill yer skinny belly! I've got everything in this pot of mine, from cat, to dog, to rook, to fairy, to them bearded dragon whatsits! Enough to sate the appetite of the Great Beast himself!'

'Did you say fairy?'

'I did indeed, every pot 'as at least eight-percent real sewer fairy – that's a Lady Labelle guarantee, that is.'

Rita suddenly didn't feel quite so hungry.

The Night Fair was a chaos of noise, of people, of smells, and Rita was having to try very hard not to become overwhelmed by it all.

Carlisle stopped suddenly, causing Rita to bump into the back of him.

'Sorry.'

'The word "sorry" is for the stupid.'

'Okay. Why have we stopped?'

'Because we are here.'

Rita looked past Carlisle at the tent before them. Its ragged canvas might once have been brightly coloured, but was now varying shades of brown. A sign above the entrance flaps said FORTUNES TOLD.

'A fortune-teller?' said Rita. 'Really? This is your big idea? How about after this we grab a paper and check our horoscopes?'

'Let me do the talking,' Carlisle replied, ignoring her shade.

'You know, technically, I'm the one heading up this investigation. I have skills in this area. Actual, tested-in-the-field skills and that.'

'How adorable. Follow me.'

They pushed through the entrance and left behind the gloom of the Night Fair for the much gloomier gloom of the fortune teller's tent. There wasn't much in the way of decoration inside. Straw covered the ground to stop the mud being churned up, and in the tent's centre was a table with a crystal ball on top. Sat behind this table, and giving Carlisle the evilest of evil eyes that Rita had ever seen, was a woman who, if Rita were to hazard a guess, was older than the oldest thing you could imagine. The fortune teller was a strip of gnarled, wrinkled leather in a kaftan and fez, a small cigar clenched between lips so thin they seemed to blink in and out of existence.

'Fuck off,' said the fortune teller, her voice a wheeze.

Carlisle chuckled. 'Now, is that any way to greet a customer, Madame Esmerelda?'

'You're not a customer, you're a lying piece of shit who should be dead and swinging from a post as a warning to other pieces of shit.'

Rita didn't need any of her training to feel the tension between the two, it was practically visible.

'I'm DS Rita Hobbes.'

'Do I look like I give a fuck, you tart?'

'Oi, I'm not a tart, you old bitch.'

'Oh? Not what the crystal ball is telling me.' She smirked and blew out a cloud of noxious smelling smoke.

'I'm not gonna be slut-shamed by a strip of jerky, thanks.'

Madame Esmerelda threw her head back and laughed. It sounded like a hoover picking up gravel.

'I'm here for information,' said Carlisle.

The fortune-teller stopped laughing and coughed so violently that Rita thought she might be choking to death, then spat out a thick glob of mucus that hit one side of the tent and slowly oozed down to the straw. As Rita watched, the glob crawled beneath the wall of the tent and away to freedom outside. Rita tried not to think too hard about that.

'Well, you're out of luck,' replied Madame Esmerelda. 'Last time I helped you, I lost a leg.'

'An unfortunate turn of events,' replied Carlisle.

'You chopped it off!'

'It seemed appropriate at the time.'

Madame Esmerelda narrowed her eyes as a rather tense silence settled over the proceedings.

'It's about a case,' Rita said at last, after it seemed like they might be stuck in an eternal, silent staring contest.

'That so?'

'Women are being taken. Murdered. By a... well, a magician.'

'And?'

'And I believe by utilising your special skills,' said Carlisle, 'you might be able to point us in the right direction.'

'I suppose he's told you his sob story?' asked the fortune teller. 'About being the rightful king and all that shit?'

'He did mention it in passing, yeah.'

'Load of old bollocks.'

'I am the rightful king,' Carlisle insisted.

'Only because you cheat at cards.'

'I never cheat.'

'You never tell the truth.'

'Regardless of how it came to be, I won the game and all that had been placed on the table was mine.'

'Right,' said Rita, 'so you're not actually royalty then. That figures.'

'Royalty?' screeched Madame Esmerelda. 'Him? I wouldn't wipe my arse with the bloke.'

Carlisle huffed and turned away from the fortune-teller.

'So why is he helping you, then?' asked the fortune-teller. 'He never helps anyone, not him. Not for no reason.'

'I have something of his,' Rita replied.

Madame Esmerelda peered into her crystal ball. 'Oh, so you've found it at last, have you?'

Carlisle grimaced and nodded.

'But she won't give it to you unless you help her out?' She began to laugh again.

'Will you help us or not?' asked Carlisle, irritated. 'Once I have regained my property, I can give you anything you please. A new leg even, if that's all it takes, you petty beast.'

'I'll not help you, Your Majesty. Why should I do anything that aids you in getting back that infernal axe of yours?'

'Because women are being murdered,' Rita cut in.

'Women die every day, you foolish thing, that's just the way of things. No, I'll not help you and I'll not help him. Now, get out of my tent.'

Carlisle turned on his heel, snapping his coat behind him, and strutted outside. Rita hovered at the exit. 'You're really not going to help? Not even try?'

'Bit of advice, dear: don't trust him. Those that do end up dead or worse, understood?'

'I can take care of myself,' Rita replied.

'You're a fool.'

'And you're a fucking bitch, love.'

Rita turned and left the tent. She found Carlisle stood brooding, staring at a popcorn machine as fresh kernels bounced within.

'So, I might be reading between the lines here,' said Rita, 'but I get the feeling that the old bag doesn't like you.'

'I should have taken more than her leg,' he hissed.

'So that's it? That's your help? I'm really impressed here. Look at my face, look at how impressed it is.'

'I will not look at your face.'

'But you're missing my impressed face.'

Carlisle grimaced. Rita grinned.

She was about to ask "what now?" when something worrying caught her eye. It was there for a second and then it was gone, but she was sure she'd seen it. Rita ducked down and peered through the popcorn stall to see beyond, and there they were.

Rabbit ears.

Large and old and tattered.

'I see them,' said Carlisle.

'What is it? Is it the magician?'

'Look away. Don't stare. Just look away and follow me as calmly as possible.'

Carlisle turned, guiding Rita to do so with one hand on her shoulder, and began to walk away from the popcorn stall.

'But he's part of it, we should go and arrest him.'

'Good idea. I take it you're tired of living and are looking for a gruesome, horrifying death?'

'Well, no.'

'Well, in that case, it's a really, really terrible idea.'

As they walked, Rita began to think she saw the rabbit ears everywhere. Poking into view from the side of a tent, reaching high from behind a man eating a hot dog, sticking up from the very ground itself.

'What's happening?' she asked.

'We have made a wrong turn,' Carlisle replied.

The ground before them split.

From the fresh crack in the earth sprouted a small figure in an old suit wearing a hedgehog mask.

'Run!' said Carlisle, and sprinted off.

Rita didn't need to be told twice. 'Wait!' she cried, as all around, every member of the Night Fair, visitor or vendor, was now either sporting a rabbit mask or a hedgehog mask.

Carlisle ducked around the side of a tent and pulled to a stop, Rita almost bashing into him. 'Who are they?'

'Mr. Spike and Mr. Cotton,' he replied.

'Right. And who are they when they're at home?'

'They are, quite literally, the stuff of nightmares.' Carlisle dropped to the ground and crossed his legs, shutting his eyes.

'Now's really not the time for a nap, mate,' she said,

peering around the edge of the tent to see the fair full of the masked pair, slowly walking towards them.

'At some point—most likely when we stepped from the fortune-teller's tent—we walked into a dreamscape created by Mr. Spike and Mr. Cotton. This is how they operate. You step into their nightmare, into a world in which they control reality.'

'Okay, that sounds bad. How bad is it?'

'Oh, it could hardly get much worse.'

'Right. Good. And what do we do?'

'If you would stop interrupting me, you would see that I'm doing it.'

'Doing what?'

Carlisle sighed, then opened one eye. 'I am concentrating. All being well, I can persuade this place to create an exit point, and we can escape.'

'And if you can't?'

'Then we die horrendously, possibly several times over.'

'Awesome.'

Rita peered around the side of the tent again as Carlisle closed his eye. The many Mr. Spikes and Mr. Cottons were almost upon them.

'Not to rush you, but you have about eight seconds.'

'Then run,' Carlisle insisted. 'It is you they are after. Hopefully, they will chase you and ignore me entirely.'

'Hopefully?'

'Run!'

'Fuck. Fuck, fuckity, fuck!'

And with that string of expletives, Rita burst from behind the tent and ran, only for the hundreds of rabbit and hedgehog mask-wearing people to charge after her, screaming. They were everywhere, and more were arriving all the time, arms bursting from the dirt like zombies crawling from the grave.

'Keep going, keep going,' said Rita, as the world around her leaned heavier and heavier into a terrifying horror movie.

It felt like the whole Night Fair was pressing in on her; like the place itself was now alive, like she could feel the dirt throbbing with its heartbeat, and it was hungry to swallow her.

As Rita zagged a corner she found herself looking into the shiny glass eyes of a rabbit mask, and in her haste to stop, stumbled and fell to the dirt.

'Detective Rita Hobbes,' said Mr. Cotton, as Mr. Spike, in his hedgehog mask, appeared at his side, 'would you like to see beneath my brother's mask?'

'No, thanks,' Rita replied, scrabbling backwards, yanking the hand axe from her belt and shaking it at the pair.

'Naughty, naughty, that does not belong to you,' said Mr. Cotton, reaching a white-gloved hand towards the axe.

'Then come get some, fuck face,' screamed Rita, swiping at his grasping fingers, staggering to her feet, and bolting once again.

'Come back, don't run. My brother Mr. Spike wishes to play.'

Every way Rita looked was blocked. There was only straight ahead, a rickety shack that proclaimed itself to be a WORLD OF MIRRORS.

'Oh, crap,' she said, fingers white-knuckling the axe. 'Any moment now would be great, Carlisle.'

Rita ran, brushed aside the strings of hanging beads that hung over the House of Mirrors' entrance, and rushed inside. Both hands gripping the axe, she backed into the place, ready to swing the blade at the first Mr. Cotton or Mr. Spike to enter, as all around mirrors of every shape and size—some whole, some horribly cracked—reflected her image back at her.

Hexed Detective

'Well?' she said. 'What are you waiting for? Come and get some, you masked dicks!'

Rita really, really hoped she sounded braver than she felt.

No one answered her challenge. Was it over? Had Carlisle done, well, whatever it was he was doing?

Rita soon got her answer as one of her reflections turned to face her. The reflection now wore a rabbit mask. Rita reflexively lashed out with the axe, smashing the mirror, causing hundreds of shards to shower the ground.

'Shit!'

'Mirror, mirror,' came Mr. Cotton's voice. 'When you were six, you used to dream about a thing that lived in the walls of the room in which you slept, Rita. Do you remember?'

Rita did remember. Remembered tucking the blanket tightly around herself so no flesh was exposed as she shook in the dark and something scritch-scratched in the walls of her orphanage room.

'You do recall, and now your skin crawls. That is me, that is us. My brother and I within each shiver, within each goose-fleshed midnight.'

Another reflection turned, this one wearing the hedgehog mask. Rita swung, smashed, stumbled back.

'Scritch-scratch, and shiver shake, do you recall the nightmares we make?'

Now it wasn't just one reflection in one mirror, it was all of them. Every reflected Rita turned to face her, all wearing the hedgehog mask of Mr. Spike.

'Let my brother dear show you what hides beneath,' said Mr. Cotton, and each of the hedgehog mask-wearing Ritas began to slowly reach up to their heads.

'Stop it!' she screeched, swinging wildly at each mirror, breaking as many as she could, but the shards now refused to remain as such, and began to run into each other like quicksilver, creating new mirrors, new reflections, and each was slowly removing a mask.

Rita ran for the exit, but now the shack seemed impossibly large, expanding and expanding, hiding the way out.

'Just look, Detective Rita Hobbes. Look at my brother, he has a special smile for you.'

Rita dropped to the ground and tried to cover her eyes, but found she couldn't close them, couldn't place her hands over them.

'He wants you to see, he wants you to. Perhaps you will see the true face of the scritch-scratch creature within your bedroom walls at last?'

The hedgehog masks, all of them, hundreds of them, began to slowly inch up, and Rita's heart bang-bang-banged in her chest. Any moment, any second, she was going to see the face beneath the mask, and she knew with a crystal clear certainty that when she did, she would lose her mind, forever.

'Stop! Please, stop!'

A hand gripped her forearm.

'Exit,' said Carlisle, and the House of Mirrors cut to black.

15

Detective Sergeant Dan Waterson was trying to remember the thing he'd forgotten.

That's not what should have been at the forefront of his mind. He was sat in the front room of a woman named Allison Mackey, a classmate of the women who had already gone missing, hoping to tease out some information that might help with the case. But there it was; the forgotten whatever-it-was, itching at his brain like a creature trying to burrow its way out.

'Are you all right, love?' asked Allison, who had been sat in uncomfortable silence for the last thirty seconds as Waterson stared glassy-eyed at the wall.

'Hm?'

'It's just, you sort of went properly quiet there for, you know, like just ages. Bit weird.'

'Right, sorry, just,' he tapped his temple with his pen, 'police brain, thinking things through. Making connections, you know.'

'Oh, like Columbo?'

'Right. Just like him. I've got a nicer coat, though.'

Allison laughed at that, and the sound of it made Waterson momentarily forget about the thing he'd forgotten.

'So, you can't think of anything that might connect the three women?'

Allison frowned and shook her head. 'No, sorry, nothing's popping up.'

'No enemies they might have? Someone they might have crossed in some way?'

'Sorry, love, it's a total blank. I didn't really know them that well. Only by name and sight, you know?'

Waterson nodded and handed Allison his card. 'If anything does occur to you, please don't hesitate to call me, okay?'

'Will do,' Allison replied, dropping the card on the mantelpiece.

'Thanks for your time.' He stood and headed for the exit.

'Sorry I couldn't be any help.'

'That's okay.' Waterson paused as he reached the door and turned back to Allison, 'One more thing.'

'Yes, Officer Columbo?' said Allison, smiling.

Waterson chuckled, then straightened up. 'Have you been experiencing any bad dreams recently?'

'Bad dreams?'

'Yeah, nightmares. Any?'

Allison frowned and shook her head. 'Nope. It's all rainbows and unicorns up here.'

Waterson nodded. 'Thanks for your help, Miss Mackey.'

As Waterson drove away, he wondered why he'd asked his final question. What did bad dreams have to do with anything? But then asking himself that brought back the fact he'd forgotten something. As he pondered the forgotten thing once again, he realised he'd parked outside of a house.

He looked at the ordinary terraced house, and wondered why he'd driven to that street and parked. He'd intended to head back to the station to type up everything he knew about the case so far. But here he was, staring at a house he was pretty sure was somehow familiar to him.

Did a friend of his live there once, maybe?

That could be it, though for the life of him he couldn't seem to match a name or even a face with the place.

Waterson shook his head, turned up the radio, and drove away.

Rita was annoyed to see her hands were still trembling as she sat behind the wheel of her car. She turned to Carlisle, sat in the passenger seat.

'What the bloody hell are those two freaks about?'

'I believe I already told you, Detective. They are the literal stuff of nightmares.'

'And they're working with the magician?'

Carlisle tapped a long, white finger against his chin and pursed his lips. 'Possibly. They are certainly on the same side at least. But Mr. Cotton and Mr. Spike are freelancers; the magician's aims are only their aims as that is the job they have been hired for. They are a selective pair though, they do not work for just anyone. If they are doing the bidding of this magician, he must be higher up the totem pole than I'd suspected.'

Carlisle looked to Rita, who tried to hide her shaking hands.

'Come,' he said, 'let us go and get a drink.'

'Best idea you've had so far,' replied Rita, and started the engine.

Big Pins was secreted down a blind alley, a side street hidden from the eyes of non-Uncanny folk, but now that Rita was of their stripe, she could see the narrow passage that had not existed to her the previous day.

'So, hidden alleyways. Cool,' she said.

'Hardly,' replied Carlisle, and strode into the blind alley towards the blinking neon sign of the tired bowling alley.

Rita followed cautiously. 'Okay, so hidden streets, bowling alleys that shouldn't be there, fairs that exist in the same place as another fair somehow; anything else?'

'Oh, lots and lots. For example, there's the Dark Lakes, or the City of the Dead underneath the streets of Manchester. Oh, and a rather nice bakery in Newcastle hidden down a nook that only eight people can see.'

'Okay, how much of that is real and how much is you taking the piss?'

'Well, where would the fun be if I told you the answer to that, Detective?'

Carlisle pushed open the door to Big Pins and entered. As Rita followed, she felt as though she had just stepped through a soap bubble.

'Ugh. What was that?'

'These sort of places—gathering spots for the Uncanny—are often situated within magic dampening bubbles. It's to stop the patrons from doing anything too dreadful to each other whilst on the premises.'

'Huh, you know that might be useful, well... anywhere booze is sold, really. We could take the idea on *Dragons' Den*, make a mint.'

'Must you prattle continuously?'

'Afraid so, Pasty Pete.'

Carlisle huffed and headed for the bar, Rita taking in the sights as she followed. As with the Night Fair, Big Pins seemed to be frequented by an eclectic bunch of people. Some looked positively regal, others would pass for homeless. In fact, she was sure she'd seen the ragged-looking man doing a little jig having bowled a strike. Hadn't she moved him along for begging in front of the cashpoint around the corner from the blind alley?

'So everyone in here is like you?' asked Rita, as she joined Carlisle at the bar.

'No need to insult me, Detective. There is nobody here quite like myself. But yes, all are of one Uncanny stripe or other. On my way through I spotted a vampire, three low-level magicians, a troll, and three dispossessed witches' familiars.'

'I'm sorry, did you just say vampire? Shouldn't we, I don't know, stab him in the heart with a stake or something?'

'Oh, wonderful, a racist as well as a simpleton.'

The conversation was brought to a premature end by the giant of a barman who appeared behind the counter, eyeing Carlisle with what looked to Rita very much like undisguised hostility.

'Back so soon?' he asked.

'Couldn't keep away, Linton. The rare ambience of this place drew me back in like an angler's lure.'

Linton snorted and began pouring drinks.

'First the fortune-teller and now this guy,' said Rita. 'Something tells me you make more enemies than friends.'

'You can always appreciate a man by the number of people who would call him their enemy.'

Rita accepted her drink from Linton and sipped as she nodded thoughtfully. 'Yeah, that sounds like bullshit to me, Pasty.'

'Please stop calling me Pasty.'

'Nope. Let's get a table.'

Rita headed for the nearest empty table as Carlisle tried to ignore the grin now plastered across Linton's face.

'Who's your friend? I like her.'

'She's a means to an end, nothing more.' Carlisle slid some cash across the bar and stalked over to Rita, his shoulders bunching as he heard Linton chuckling.

'I've got a question,' said Rita as Carlisle swept the tail of his purple coat aside and lowered himself onto a stool.

'Oh? You do surprise me.'

'If rabbit and hedgehog man can create these dream wotsits—'

'Dreamscapes—'

'Right, those wotsits, how do we know we're not in one right now? Dreamscape inside a dreamscape. You know, *Inception* shit.'

'*Inception*?'

'What? Get stuffed, you must have seen *Inception*.'

'I will not get stuffed.'

'Dreamscape inside a dreamscape; how'd you know we're not?'

'We're not.'

'How do you know?'

'Is anyone sporting a rancid old animal mask attempting to do anything awful to us?'

'No.'

'There you go then,' said Carlisle.

They sat in silence for a few seconds as Rita peered around Big Pins, looking to see if any familiar rabbit ears were poking into view.

'Aha! There's the very fellow,' said Carlisle, waving at a man who had just entered Big Pins and, by the looks of things, was trying to slip right back out again before Carlisle spotted him.

The man, if it was a man—Rita was wary to jump to

Hexed Detective

such conclusions, now—shuffled over. He wore distressed-looking clothes and fingerless gloves, and his face looked a little, well... *moley*. If you were on the bus and he got on, you'd have everything crossed that he wouldn't take the seat next to you.

'Carlisle,' said Formby, his sharp front teeth yellowed and jutting out.

'You've got, like, Spock ears,' said Rita, peering at Formby's pointed protuberances.

'You must forgive the woman,' said Carlisle, 'her keen detective eyes never sleep when faced with the blindingly obvious.'

Formby smiled a sharp-toothed smile at Rita and bowed his head a little. 'Detective Rita Hobbes, I am your servant.'

'Hey, how did you know my name?'

'I am an eaves. It is my business to know, well, everyone's business.'

Formby shuffled on to a spare stool and began to drink Carlisle's pint.

'This is Formby,' said Carlisle, 'his sorry ilk sell secrets for a sniff of magic. They have little loyalty and are, as you can see, quite uncommonly hideous to look at. Think of him as that rarest of things: a useful junkie.'

'As far as introductions go, that was about as rude as it gets,' said Rita.

'No, I refrained from mentioning his rancid odour.'

'Fair enough.'

'So, did you find your magician?' asked Formby.

'Not yet, though I did make the acquaintance of a couple of friends of his. You failed to mention the presence of Mr. Cotton and Mr. Spike in your fair town, eaves. A regretful oversight on your part, I'm sure.'

Formby shrank into himself a little. 'I don't like to say

their names. If you speak of them too often, they appear in your dreams.'

'Superstitious nonsense.'

'It's true!'

'If you know all the secrets of Blackpool,' said Rita, 'how come you don't know who this magician bastard is?'

'I don't know everything, I just know a lot, is all. Something must be spoken and shared from person to person for it to pass my ears, and no one who I mix with, pass by, or lurk close to has spoken anything of use.'

'Did I say a "useful junkie"?' said Carlisle. 'My mistake. Now if you'll excuse me, I must make use of the little boys' room.' He rose and strode across Big Pins towards the toilets.

'Carlisle,' said Rita, leaning over to Formby, 'what is he? I mean, he's not really a person, is he?'

Formby glanced over his shoulder to make sure Carlisle was gone. 'No, not a man. No one knows quite what he is, but he's not to be trusted.'

'Unfortunately for me, I don't have much choice. Not until this hex bullshit is gone and the murderer's stopped, anyway. Then he can have his stupid axe back, and I can get on with my normal, boring, awesome life.'

'Can I... can I see it?'

'See what?'

'The artefact. The thing he craves. The axe.'

Rita shrugged. 'Yeah, suppose so.'

Formby chittered his teeth together and clapped in excitement, his pointed ears twitching as Rita reached beneath her coat and discovered that she didn't actually have the axe anymore.

'Bastard... bastard!' Rita sprinted to the mens' toilets, startling a man with three eyes as he relieved himself at the urinal.

Carlisle was nowhere to be seen.

'Bastard!'

She burst back into the bar area, Formby there waiting.

'Told you, never trust. Never, never.'

Formby scampered at Rita's heel as she raced across the room to the exit, ready to tear up the streets in search of the fleeing Carlisle, only to almost trip over him as she ran into the blind alley.

Carlisle was laid out on the cobbles, flat on his back, unconscious, the axe on the ground beside him.

'Sneaky bloody bastard,' said Rita. She walked back into Big Pins, collected what remained of her drink, walked back out, and poured the drink over Carlisle's face.

'Whugrnyuh,' said Carlisle, or at least something to that effect, as the beer shower snapped him back into consciousness.

'Morning,' said Rita, picking up the axe and sliding it back into her belt beneath her coat, as Formby sniggered. 'What do you think you were playing at?' she asked.

'Well, you just took it without being given permission by its wielder, I thought it might proffer me the same courtesy as a previous owner,' said Carlisle, pulling a hankie from an inside pocket as he stood and wiped at his foamy, damp face.

'And how did that work out for you?'

'Not well, apparently,' replied Carlisle, giving Formby, who was now almost bent double with laughter, the evil eye.

'Try that again,' said Rita, 'and the deal is finished, right? If we're partners in this, then we've got to have each other's back.'

'Well,' said Formby, almost unable to get the words out, 'His Majesty here ended up *on* his back at least.' Formby threw back his head and cackled.

'That does not even work as a joke,' replied a sour Carlisle.

'On his back!' repeated Formby, tears streaming.

'Detective, please inform this foul, ugly creature that if he keeps on laughing I'll make earrings from his withered genitals.'

Formby shut his mouth and did his best to prevent any further smirks from escaping.

16

The Magician hated hospitals.

He was now twenty years old, and had spent more than enough time over the last few years sat within the walls of places like this. Pale corridors and tired chairs, disinfectant stink, and the *beep-beep* of sad machines.

He shivered, or more accurately, he trembled. A tremor that turned his hands blurry.

'Be brave,' said the constant voice at his ear. Said the Angel of Blackpool.

His mother was dying.

He remembered the first time he heard the Angel's voice, knelt down on the beach, digging a hole in the sand, trying to ignore his mother as she cried. He'd give just about anything for there to be enough life left in her for tears.

The door to her room opened and a doctor stepped out. The Magician thought he looked like a bird; a pinched face and hook nose.

'She's not long left now,' said the doctor, and the Magician dug his nails into the palms of his hands to stop himself from smashing this bird in the face.

'Be brave,' said the Angel.

He smiled and nodded and the doctor walked off down the corridor, the Magician's cold eyes watching him until he turned out of view.

'I could kill him,' he said.

'Yes. You could kill everyone in this hospital,' replied the Angel.

He smiled at that.

'Yes. I could send them one by one by one into the sea, just like Nelson. Someone would walk along the beach, with a metal detector maybe—some sad, useless old man full of life he's no use for—and he'd see them all. See all the bodies floating on the water's surface like grim lily pads.'

He walked to the open door of his mother's hospital room and paused, fingertips brushing against the door handle.

'Why don't I do that? Just send them all to sea and not go in this room at all.'

'Because that would be the end and you know we have much more important work. A destiny, you and I. We're meant for great things.'

The Magician nodded, then stepped inside the hospital room. His mother was laid out in the single bed, a thin cotton sheet over her. Her face was thin, cheeks shallow. She'd lost so much weight over the last few months that she barely looked like his mother at all. This was a stranger. A thing. Trying to think of her like that helped him not to scream.

He pulled a chair over to her bedside. He didn't look at her. Instead, he looked at the window on the far wall. He could see the sky through it; the brightest blue with barely a wisp of cotton floating through.

'Where is Heaven?' he asked.

'Not there,' replied the Angel. 'Not in the bright blue sky.

Not beyond it, either. Heaven exists elsewhere. Other. Aside from. Apart.'

His mother gurgled, a wet rattle in her throat.

First his dad, and now his mum, taken cruelly and before their time.

'God cares not for your tears. Cares not about the pain He has caused. An indifferent monster, that is what God is. That is the great truth hidden by those with something to gain from the pretence, in their houses of gold and shame.'

'When can we start?' asked the Magician.

'It is almost time. The first step we take today, at last.'

The Magician smiled, even as the *beep-beep-beep* of the sad machine became one long *beeeeeeeeeeeeeeeeeeeeeep* and the creature he could not believe was truly his mum finally ceased her nauseating, shallow-breathed gurgle, and what lived in her left the cramped hospital room behind.

Nurses entered and attended to her, said words to the Magician that he didn't hear. He stood and walked through the fog, down the hospital corridors, past room after room of those ignored by God. Left to die slowly.

Soon, he found himself staring through a large window at a room full of newborn babies, wriggling in their cots. New life. New death. More lambs to the slaughter before the chilling indifference of their creator.

In the room beyond the glass, the newborn children were not alone. Two men stood in old dusty suits, facing the Magician. One wore a rabbit mask, the other a hedgehog mask.

'They are here,' said the Angel in his ear.

'Who are they?' he asked, looking from Mr. Cotton to Mr. Spike, a shiver running down his spine.

'They are believers in our undertaking. They have gifts of their own, which, when combined with my power, can be turned to our advantage.'

As the Magician watched, black smoke began to stream from the eyeholes of the masks. The black smoke weaved like snakes above the cots, moving from each, until six of the children were selected and the smoke wiggled into the children through their eyes, their noses, their mouths.

'These six,' said the Angel, 'they are anointed by me through Mr. Cotton and Mr. Spike. The magic placed inside of them, the taste of their dark dream, shall ripen as they age, and when the time is right, each shall be harvested with the artefact.'

The Magician thought about his dad, about his mum.

'Why can't I take them now? I can get the axe and finish them.'

'Patience. I have huddled trapped beneath the sea for centuries. There is no rush. My touch, through Mr. Spike and Mr. Cotton's dark dreamings, must fuse with their souls fully over the coming years, or their sacrifice will mean nothing.'

The Magician was impatient. His anger boiled within him. But the Angel was right. It never lied to him. He would wait. Their time would come. The time when he would take his axe to each of them. The time when he and the Angel of Blackpool would face God and punish Him for His sins.

17

Rita killed the engine as she and Carlisle pulled to a stop in front of a pleasant-looking semi-detached house.

'I think this is it,' she said, pulling out her notebook and double-checking the address.

'Must we?' asked Carlisle.

'Well, if you have any other leads like the fortune-teller who hates your guts and won't tell us a bloody thing, let's go and see them, 'cos that wasn't a massive waste of time at all.'

Carlisle pursed his lips.

'Or we could do some proper detective work and start interviewing this list of known classmates of the missing women. How about that?'

Rita got out of the car. 'Oi,' she said, leaning down to see Carlisle, 'are you gonna keep sulking, or should we get on with this?'

Carlisle huffed, then stepped out of the car. 'I do not sulk. I brood.'

'You also nick stuff from your partner and try to leg it away.'

'You realise I could pin you like a butterfly and pluck out your limbs one by one?'

'Yeah, and you realise I could take your axe and shove it up your arse?'

'Touché. Obviously this woman will not be able to see or hear you, so I shall take the lead.'

'Okay, but listen to what I have to say, right? I have actual training in this stuff.'

'I look forward to being wowed by your staggering interview skills, Detective.' Carlisle rang the doorbell.

There were twenty-eight names on the list, including the three women who had so far gone missing. Twenty-eight classmates who moved through school together. Of the twenty-five who weren't the missing women, only ten had remained in Blackpool, and it was these ten that Carlisle and Rita intended to visit, one by one.

As luck would have it, they struck gold with visit number one: Wanda Radcliffe, a plump woman with a giant mane of dark blonde curls. She peered at the card Carlisle offered, the card that was very definitely not police identification, and waved him and the invisible-to-her-eyes Rita through to the kitchen.

'Oh, aye, I've heard all about it,' said Wanda. 'I'm still mates with a couple of people from school and we've been messaging non-stop on Facebook.'

'I'm sure it's all very exciting,' said Carlisle.

'Oh, it is! I mean, sad and that, obvs, but exciting too. You never think this sort of thing'll happen to people you sort of know, do you?'

Carlisle smiled thinly.

'Ask about grudges,' prompted Rita.

'I will,' replied Carlisle.

'What's that?' asked Wanda.

'The three women that have been abducted, do you have

any information about someone that may have a reason to dislike them? A grudge?'

'Oh, yeah, Mister Nolan.'

'Who's that?' asked Rita. 'Wait, you ask,' she said, nudging Carlisle.

'And Mister Nolan would be?'

'Oh, this perv of a maths teacher. Was always leaning over you, just a bit too close, you know? Looking down your shirt. He eventually made a pass at Jane. Jane Bowan. Squeezed her tit, so she said. Her and a bunch of her friends went to the Head and Mister Nolan got the sack. I'd say he's probably pissed off with them.'

'Ha! There we go, we do a bit of proper police work and we get an actual lead. Weird that, eh?' said Rita.

Carlisle ignored her smug smile.

Waterson was sat at his desk at the station, idly doodling in the margins of a newspaper.

'Oi, dickhead!'

Waterson looked up to see DS Nation, a colleague with a year-round tan who swore he never went near a sunbed, waving at him.

'Hm? What?'

'For the third time, you coming down for a few pints later or what?'

'Right, yeah. Probably.'

'What's wrong with your face?' asked Nation.

Waterson sat up straight. 'Do you ever get the feeling that you're missing something? Something big?'

'Is this your way of confessing you've got one of them micro-dicks, mate?'

That got a big laugh from the office. Dick jokes always did.

'Yes. that's it. I thought you'd be the person to go to about it. Idiot.'

Waterson went back to his doodle. He was scritch-scratching a pair of rabbit ears, over and over.

'Anything useful yet?' asked DCI Jenner, peering at Waterson's doodles. 'Hard at work, I see, Waterson.'

'Yep, sorry Guv, just, you know, thinking things through.'

'By drawing Playboy bunnies? What about the case? You got anything?'

'Not yet, but I've only been to see two of the other classmates so far. Something will turn up.'

'Hm. It had better. Upstairs is on me like a bastard about this. They've got the press hounding them every two minutes, so give me something I can take to them and make it soon, right?'

'Yes, Guv, will do,' replied Waterson with more confidence than he felt.

As Jenner set off towards his office, Waterson stopped him and pointed to a vacant desk opposite his own. 'Guv, whose desk is that?'

'Hm?' DCI Jenner looked at the empty desk and his brow creased. 'Well, that's… um… I don't think anyone's used that for a few years, have they?'

'Nope,' said Nation, chiming in.

'Right. Of course. That's what I thought,' said Waterson.

DCI Jenner looked at the desk for a second more, then shook his head. 'Right, no rest for the wicked. Back to it, Waterson. Get me something useful.'

Waterson looked at the empty desk, then back to his rabbit ear doodles. 'Yes, Guv. Will do.'

A ping from his computer caught his attention, a new

email from Nation. 'SPURT: PILL GUARANTEES YOU AN EXTRA THREE INCHES!'

Waterson deleted the email and offered a middle finger to the guffawing Nation.

Mister Derek Nolan, former Head of Maths at Old Lane Secondary School, currently assistant manager at a local supermarket. The picture of him that Rita had found did not make him look like a fearsome magician capable of consorting with dream monsters and chopping up innocent women with an axe. The picture showed a rather meek-looking man with thinning hair and a bushy moustache.

'What do you think?' she asked, wagging the picture under Carlisle's aquiline nose.

'That one should never judge a book by its cover.'

After his third knock on the door failed to rouse an occupant, it became clear that Mister Nolan was not at home.

'Come on, we can wait in the car,' said Rita.

'Or we can just go inside to see what might be found.'

'Yeah, that's sort of against the law.'

'Most of the best ideas are.' Carlisle crouched and placed the side of his face against the door.

'What are you doing? Can you hear someone in there?'

'I am attempting to persuade the door to unlock itself.'

'Course you are, you skinny nut-bag.'

Carlisle sighed. 'Could you please hush that mouth of yours for a few short seconds? This is a delicate waltz I am undertaking, and it requires the utmost concentration.'

Rita put up both hands and stepped back. 'Go for it, weirdo; you sweet talk that sexy door.'

Carlisle closed his eyes and placed the palm of one hand

over the lock. After ten silent seconds, at which point Rita had just about reached the maximum amount of time her mouth was willing to remain silent, the locking mechanism clicked.

'Et voilà,' he said, grinning and bouncing to his feet.

'Get to fuck. No way.'

Carlisle pushed open the now unlocked door. 'As I believe you moronic types like to retort, "*Yes, way*". Shall we?' Carlisle stepped across the threshold. Rita glanced over both shoulders to see if she was being watched, remembered that she was invisible, and was glad Carlisle hadn't seen her do it. She scooted into Mister Nolan's house.

Inside, it was clear that Mister Nolan lived alone. The sort of man who would feel up a teenager's chest was rarely a catch for full-grown women. The rooms were sparsely dressed and worn. The decor had not been updated in at least ten years. Everything was faded and tatty, and Rita could almost smell the loneliness. That and the other man smells. He really needed to crack a window in that place.

'Do you sense it?' asked Carlisle, emerging from the kitchen, his eyes seeming to glow a pale yellow in the gloom.

'Yeah, this guy is bloody tragic. He needs to invest in some industrial-strength air freshener, like, immediately, if not sooner.'

'Not the unpleasant, musty odour and general funk of tragedy; the magic.'

'Magic?'

'Oh yes.'

'And what does that feel like?'

'Like... potential.' He made his way to a small wooden door beneath the stairs. 'Down there. It is stronger down there.'

'What are you saying? Mister Nolan the boob-squeezer is magic?'

'No, I am saying that the magic within this house is not just the expected background amount, but that it has been used. Drawn upon. And often. So we investigate.'

Carlisle opened the small door and ducked inside. Rita took the axe from under her coat and followed him. She'd expected little more than a small, cramped cupboard. Instead, she found Carlisle descending a set of worn stone steps. Not the kind of worn stone steps you'd find in a house, but the kind you might see Indiana Jones descending, right before he was chased by a huge rolling boulder.

'Okay, nothing to worry about here,' said Rita, fingers flexing around the wooden handle of the axe.

As she made her way down the steps, making sure not to fall too far behind Carlisle, she had a similar feeling to the one she had when she entered the stone corridor hidden in the arcade.

'This definitely fits with the other hidden place, hey?' she said.

'It is similar, I agree,' replied Carlisle, running a finger along a stone wall and licking his fingertip.

'Gross,' said Rita.

Carlisle spat on the steps.

'Grosser.'

'Hm, this is not the same level of magic, but it is, perhaps, still a little too coincidental.'

Rita joined Carlisle at the bottom of the steps and peered up to see the light from the house, still just about visible.

'If this guy is a super-duper magician, how much danger are we in exactly?'

'If he is the man responsible for the abductions, we could barely be in greater danger.'

'Great. Thanks for the confidence booster.'

Carlisle walked forward, almost seeming to drift, his heavy boots light on the stone floor. By comparison, Rita's own footsteps sounded like a heavy metal drum solo. The space at the bottom of the stairs was cramped, with flickering torches clamped to the rough walls.

'Atmospheric, eh?' said Rita.

'Magicians do like to set a scene,' replied Carlisle, as he approached the wooden door set into the far wall. He gripped the metal ring at its centre, glanced back to Rita with a nod, then pulled.

The door creaked outwards, the noise setting Rita's teeth on edge as she clenched and re-clenched the axe.

'Behind me,' said Carlisle.

'No worries. If he's in there, you're welcome to get hit first, mate.'

Carlisle smiled, then stepped into the room, Rita wary at his heels.

Inside, there was not a dingy sacrifice chamber, like at the games arcade, but rather a giant study that would not have looked out of place at Hogwarts.

'Shit,' said Rita, 'I think we just broke into Dumbledore's man cave.'

The room was huge, with plush carpeting and fine wooden bookcases that stretched up for three impossible storeys, sliding sets of brass ladders giving access to the highest shelves.

'Uh, that's sort of not possible, right? If this place was as tall as those bookcases, it'd be jutting out the top of the house.'

'Bigger on the inside than out,' said Carlisle.

'Okay, so maybe it's Doctor Who's man cave.'

At the centre of the room was a large oak desk with a green leather chair sat behind it. Dominating the table was a giant, ancient-looking book, its leather cover now ragged with age.

'What are all these books, then?'

Carlisle ran his fingers over the open pages of the volume on the table, then peered at the shelves packed tight with book after book.

'Magical texts. Rare, some of them. If we took just a few I've spotted, we could make enough money to live like sultans for eternity.'

'Yeah, we're not on the rob, so keep your hands off.'

'Just an idle thought.'

Rita snorted and flopped into the leather chair as she took a look at the book open on the desk. It looked like the ancient bibles that monks used to delicately transcribe, but with much stranger pictures. Not of saints, or angels, but of internal organs, and animals with their throats slashed and their blood dripping into a cauldron.

'What language is that?' Rita asked. 'Latin or something?'

'Hm? No, that is a language much older than Latin. Much, much older, from a people you will not find mention of in any of your history books. A lost people who knew the power of words and sounds.'

'Why aren't they remembered?'

'Their island was lost beneath the waves millennia ago.'

'Wait… are you talking about Atlantis? Are these Atlantis words!'

'It's always Atlantis with you people. No, it's not Atlantis.'

'Aw.' Rita slumped back, sulking.

It was then that she noticed the man stood in the doorway.

'Bastards!' said Mister Nolan.

'We'd like a word with you, magician,' said Carlisle. He opened his mouth to speak again but was stopped by the purple lightning that burst from Mister Nolan's fingers and struck him in the chest, sending him crashing into one of the bookcases.

'Shit!' Rita ran to him, but Carlisle was already back on his feet and running for the door after the fleeing Nolan. 'Wait up!' she yelled, giving chase.

As she made it up the stone steps and out of the cupboard under the stairs, she was just in time to see Nolan pull a dagger out of thin air and toss it at Carlisle, who swept his hands to the side, somehow pushing the knife off course so that it embedded itself up to the hilt in the wooden door, two inches from Rita's face.

'Shitting hell!' she said, almost dropping the axe.

'You cannot run from me, magician,' said Carlisle, his long coat billowing out dramatically even though Rita was pretty sure there was no wind coming from anywhere.

'Wrong,' replied Nolan, clapping his hands together, making the air behind him ripple and warp.

'Quick!' said Carlisle, grabbing Rita's arm and yanking her forward as Nolan leapt through the warping air and disappeared.

'Where'd he go?' asked Rita.

'Let's see,' replied Carlisle, pulling her into the strange, rippling air just as it collapsed.

It turned out that where Mister Nolan had gone was Blackpool Pier. Rita stumbled as the pier appeared around her, and she fell to her knees, the axe skittering across the ground as she dropped.

'I feel sick,' she said.

'Transportation magic. It can do that if you're not used to it,' replied Carlisle, who had stepped from the portal and on to the pier as elegantly as if he had stepped from one room to another.

Rita pushed herself up on shaky legs and retrieved the axe. They were on the North Pier, the longest of the town's three piers; the one with a theatre crouched at its far end. Over the decades it had played host to any number of pantomimes, novelty acts, and mostly-forgotten comedians. Rita had vague memories of being taken to see Cannon & Ball there once as a child, a comic duo briefly and inexplicably popular in the 1980s who clung on to work in places like Blackpool.

'I think it's safe to say that our Mister Nolan has something to hide,' said Rita, gulping down a burp that tasted like the previous day's dinner.

'Reasonably safe, yes. If you are going to vomit, please do it over the side of the pier and into the sea.'

'I'm not going to vom—' Rita ran to the side of the pier and hung over the railings, loudly emptying her stomach.

'Are you quite finished?'

Rita straightened up, wiping the sleeve of her coat across her mouth. 'Better out than in.'

'You disgust me.'

Rita burped. 'So where's Mister Nolan?'

'He's here. I can feel him.'

Rita looked up and down the deserted pier. 'Actually, where is anyone? At all? There's always people on the pier.'

Carlisle walked towards the theatre, and Rita hustled to catch up.

'Well? Where is everyone? Actually, why can't I hear any birds? Normally you can barely think around here for all the seagull squawking.'

'It seems Mister Nolan has taken us to a moment between moments.'

'Yeah, what's that mean, then?'

'He has made a jump into a pocket of stationary time where he believes he could hide until he was safe. Sadly for him, I was able to follow the path before it degraded.'

Rita patted him on the shoulder. 'Good work, partner.'

Carlisle stopped walking. 'Never pat me again.'

'You got it, Creepy.'

Carlisle continued walking.

Inside, the theatre was not just silent, it was almost as though the entire place was holding its breath to avoid drawing attention to itself. The place was oppressively, noisily silent. Rita looked at the dirty carpet with its cigarette burns and worn-in dirt. Carlisle sniffed at the air.

'This way.'

'Yes, sir,' replied Rita, saluting and almost chopping herself in the face with the axe.

'Cretin.'

They made their way through to the theatre itself, with row upon row of empty seats facing the stage.

'Really?' said Carlisle, his voice projecting effortlessly around the large room. 'A little dramatic to stage a last stand on a *literal* stage, is it not?'

'Leave me alone, Carlisle,' came a reply.

'Mister Nolan?' said Rita. 'Why so nervy? We just want to ask you a few friendly questions.'

They moved down the aisle towards the stage, its red velvet curtain down.

'You broke into my home, and then into my inner sanctum.'

'Sanctum?' said Carlisle, snorting, 'a true magician's sanctum would not be stepped into so easily. But you're no true magician, are you?'

'He seems to know his stuff, to me,' said Rita.

'Yes, but you are a clueless buffoon.'

'Point to you, carry on.'

'Stop!' said Mister Nolan. 'No closer, Carlisle, or you'll regret it!'

'I see my reputation precedes me again.'

'I've heard the stories. The whispers. The accusations.'

'And we've heard accusations about you,' said Rita.

Hexed Detective

The curtain ruffled and Mister Nolan stepped out. Both of his hands appeared to be on fire.

'Holy shit!' said Rita.

Nolan raised a hand then punched it forward, the flames rushing towards her and forcing Rita to dive out of the way, landing painfully on a row of seats.

'Bastard! Ow.'

She scrambled up to see Carlisle rushing the stage as Nolan clapped his hands together and a multi-coloured glow formed around his fists, which then shot towards Carlisle.

'Watch out!'

Carlisle crouched and lifted his coat to cover his face, the magic-whatever-it-was struck the coat and deflected away, straight for Rita. No time to move aside, Rita swung out at the ball of crackling, coloured light and struck it sweetly with the axe head and—

Rita blinked and was happy to see she was neither dead nor harmed. But something had happened. Something new.

She could feel it.

Feel what Mister Nolan had attacked Carlisle with, and what he'd deflected into her path.

Magic.

Rita could hear it talking to her. Could feel it prickling like static across her skin. Could taste it in her mouth.

'What spell are you?' she asked or thought or felt or maybe screamed. The colours of the universe strobed across her vision and she could see the very fabric of the spell cast. Could see the stitches that bound it into the shape and purpose Mister Nolan had commanded of it. It wasn't a spell meant to kill, meant to destroy; rather it was a concussive blast meant to render Rita and Carlisle unconscious.

'You're mine, now,' Rita told the spell, and she could almost sense it wag its non-existent tail in obedience.

'Rita?' said Carlisle, his voice distant, muffled, as the

147

magic rolled and rushed inside of her, then rushed into the axe.

'Heads up, dickless!' said Rita, which wasn't exactly a standard wizard incantation, but it did the trick.

The spell now had a new master and a new destination. Rita swung the axe, its metal head molten for the blink of an eye, and the magic, a rippling spear of blues and oranges and colours that no ordinary person had ever seen, burst forth and shot towards Mister Nolan, whose face was wide with shock.

The spell struck him in the chest, and Mister Nolan flew through the air, slid backwards across the wooden stage of the theatre then came to a stop, quite unconscious.

There was a silent pause as Rita looked from the prone Mister Nolan to the axe in her hands, and then to Carlisle. 'Well… bloody, bastarding, hell! That was amazing!'

Carlisle snorted and headed over to the out-cold Mister Nolan, hopping up on to the stage like a cat.

'Oh, come on! Did you see that shit? I totally caught his magic and twatted him with it. Somehow. Just like at the arcade. Only this time I really felt it. Really saw it.'

'The artefact. My artefact,' said Carlisle. 'I told you, it gives each wielder a different gift. It appears, in your case, that it allows you to take another's ability and use it against them.'

Rita grinned wildly, passing the axe from hand to hand, throwing in a few swings for good measure. 'Brilliant. Awesome. Ooh, so, if, like, someone is really good at piano, could I tap them with this axe and suddenly shit all over Jerry Lee Lewis?'

'Is Jerry Lee Lewis magic?'

'He can play piano with his feet, so yeah, sort of.'

'Then perhaps.'

Rita scampered down the aisle and clambered on to the

stage to join Carlisle, who was standing over the unconscious Mister Nolan.

'So what now?' she asked.

'Now we bind him, we wake him, and we interrogate him.'

'Right, good. On board with all that.'

'And then we shall kill him.'

'Slightly less on board.'

18

It had been thirty years since the Magician's mother died, slowly and painfully, in hospital. Thirty years since he watched Mr. Cotton and Mr. Spike stand over the newborn babies and infect them with darkness.

Thirty long, awful years.

'Our wait is over, friend,' said the Angel of Blackpool, and the Magician hastily wiped a tear from his eye before it had a chance to fall and draw anyone's attention.

'At last, at last,' he said under his breath, fingers stroking his calendar, the day circled in red.

'Revenge,' said the Angel.

'Revenge,' said the Magician.

He left work early, said his goodbyes as normal, and drove home.

Jane Bowan. She was going to be the first. The start. Step one to gaining the power to free the Angel and shatter the doors to Heaven.

Revenge.

The Magician realised he was actually whistling as he collected his bags and placed them in the boot of his car.

One contained his robes, his mask; the other contained the axe. The axe he discovered on the beach so very long ago.

He drove to the arcade, retrieved his bags from the back of his car, and wandered through, past the hordes of kids, tourists, and locals who were rushing around, moving from game to game, full of noise and flashing lights and chaos.

No one paid any attention to him as he slipped through into the stockroom. The staff at the arcade were so wishy-washy that the concealment magic he employed was probably not even necessary; he could have walked through, bold as brass. But now was not the time to risk arousing suspicion. The work was too important. Too longed for.

He made his way past the giant bags full of stuffed toys and opened the door that only he could see, stepping through into the coolness of the stone corridor beyond. The stone corridor led to a chamber. A point of power. Two times pressed together like the pages of a book. This point was a weak spot in reality; a tangling of mystical nerves, where the sacrifice to come would be impregnated with even more meaning, more power, more wonder.

Jane Bowan was waiting for him. She was unconscious, laid out on top of a large grey stone, her ankles and wrists manacled tightly to it so she could not leave, could not even move her arms or legs. Trapped. Pinned like a butterfly.

He moved to the back of the chamber and unzipped the first bag, retrieving the axe and placing it gently on the small altar.

'Can you feel it?' asked the Angel.

'I feel it.'

And he did. The power in that room. The hushed, awed expectation of the journey they were finally undertaking. He'd had to wait so long. So long for the touch of Mr. Cotton and Mr. Spike, imbued with the Angel's magic, to fully bloom within each person chosen. It had wormed its way through their bones. Their muscles. Their souls. Infected even their dreams. Fear was important. It might seem cruel, but fear leavens the sacrifice. It had all been explained to him.

Fear was important.

He remembered how scared he'd been when he'd heard his mother's anguished, animal cries when his dad's body had been discovered.

Fear was important.

The Magician opened the second bag and pulled out his scarlet robes. He marvelled at how the material seemed to shine beneath the flames that flickered at the torch heads. He slipped the robe over his head, his arms, and let it fall into place over him. The soft material caressed his skin and almost seemed to sigh as he stroked his palms over it.

'This is the first,' he said. 'This is the first. There will be six. The axe will come down and then we shall take what's His.'

'I almost wish God knew what was coming for Him. The fury. The anger. The power,' said the Angel, and it made the Magician smile. 'Knew the righteous anger that will lay waste to His kingdom of absence, and scorch him from existence.'

The Magician pulled out the mask and looked into its empty eyes. He touched the goat skin that was stretched over it. Stroked the curled horns.

'I hide my face from God as I do this, not out of fear, but out of contempt.'

He placed the goat mask over his head and reached for the axe. He felt the weight of it in his hand. Felt the right and the might in his heart.

Revenge.

'Where... where am I?' asked Jane Bowan, her voice groggy as she awoke.

The Magician didn't answer at first as he did not hear her.

All he heard was the rasp of his heavy breath against the inside of the mask and his own heartbeat thumping against his chest. A tattoo of anxiety. He flexed his fingers around the handle of the axe. His hands were sweaty, he realised they were trembling.

'Fear is natural, fear is right,' said the Angel. 'Do not let it sway you.'

'Where am I?' repeated Jane Bowan, her voice now a scream of panic.

The Magician walked forward until he was within her sight. She shook and wriggled and fought against the chains, her eyes wide and rolling with panic. Terror. Disbelief.

Mr. Cotton and Mr. Spike had delivered her to him. Now it was his turn.

'Please! Please don't, please don't,' she begged.

The Magician felt his knees wobble.

'Do not falter. Do not weaken.'

'Is this... is this right?' asked the Magician.

'Let me go! Help! Somebody help, please!'

The Magician lowered the axe and walked away. Wanted to pull off the mask, needed to breathe a little freer. Didn't want his own hot breath bouncing back into his face.

'Listen to me,' said the Angel.

'I can't,' he replied, 'I'm sorry. I thought I could. I wanted to. This is... it's too difficult.'

'Please don't hurt me,' said Jane Bowan. 'Please. I'll do anything. You don't... you don't have to do this, I won't tell anyone, I won't, I promise, please.'

'This is not murder,' said the Angel.

The Magician felt the heft of the axe.

'This is not murder. This is a blessing. Her life will mean something. Something wonderful. Think of all the other people who perish because of God's neglect. Think of the other children who lose their parents in the face of His monstrous indifference.'

The Magician turned to Jane Bowan, his face a hidden grimace, teeth clenched, a high-pitched whine escaping from between them.

'Please don't,' she said.

'It has to stop,' said the Angel. 'It has to. You know that.'

'I know that. I know.'

'This, in the end, is a kindness. A kindness to all of those that we will save. If she knew the truth of it, if it could be explained properly, she would thank you.'

The Magician straightened up, his teeth unclenched, his palms no longer sweating.

He saw the millions starving around the world.

'Please.'

He saw an earthquake that shook bridges and buildings and roads to dust, killing hundreds. Thousands.

'Don't.'

He saw his mother, laid out in a hospital bed, her face unrecognisable.

'We're going to make Him pay,' said the Angel. 'It's time to go to work.'

The Magician smiled. He'd faltered, but that was only because he was good and true.

He swung the axe above his head and brought it down in one swift, efficient move. The deed was done.

Jane Bowan was dead.

The Magician laughed. Just once. That hadn't been so bad.

Jane Bowan's spirit, her soul, sat up out of her body. It sparkled as though made of fairy dust.

'What's happening?' She looked down at her own dead body and screamed, fell from the stone, and scrambled backwards along the ground.

'One more swing,' said the Magician.

He stepped towards the soul of Jane Bowan and swung the axe. As the head met her insubstantial body, Jane Bowan twisted and rippled and shook, and was absorbed into the axe itself.

And then it was all over.

He placed the axe on the altar and pulled off the goat head mask. The cool air felt good against his skin as he hung his head back and took deep, cold breaths.

'I am proud,' said the Angel.

'For my dad. For my mother. I do this for you.'

'We do this for all. For every child who's ever wept in the dark because of *Him*.'

The Magician felt a tear running down his cheek, but it wasn't a tear of sadness or fear. No. It was joy.

At last, at last.

'We are so close,' said the Angel of Blackpool.

Revenge.

19

Mister Nolan's eyes snapped open as the cold water punched him in the face.

'Wakey, wakey, Mister Gropey,' said Rita.

Nolan tried to stand, then realised he was tied to a chair in the front row of a theatre.

'Let me go!' he yelled, water spraying comically from his thick greying moustache.

'Hush, or I will crack your skull beneath my boot,' said Carlisle, sat on the edge of the stage, legs dangling.

Rita pulled out her badge and waggled it in front of Mister Nolan's face. 'That's right, Magic Mike, you're nicked.'

'For what?'

'Well, for one thing, you threw all that magic stuff at me, a police officer, so that's assault.'

'You broke into my home!'

'Okay, true, but it was all for a good cause.'

Carlisle hopped off the stage and walked towards Mister Nolan, who attempted to push himself back through the solid chair at his approach.

'Women are being murdered in this dreadful town of yours, Nolan. Murdered by a magician.'

'What's that gotta do with me?'

'Jane Bowan,' said Rita. 'Ellie Mason. Gemma Wheeler. Any of those names sound, ooh, I dunno, a little familiar?' Rita mimed groping in front of Mister Nolan's widening eyes.

'I… okay, yes, I know them, they were pupils of mine.'

'Pupils who assisted in your firing,' said Carlisle, 'and now a magician appears to be picking them off one by one, and would you look at this, a man who would have spent years blowing on the embers of his grudge to keep it nice and hot turns out to have developed into a rather basic but effective magician.'

'Quite the coincidence, that,' replied Rita.

'Oh, the word coincidence is written in ten-foot, flashing neon letters above his head, Detective.'

Mister Nolan glanced above his head, as if the neon letters might actually be there.

'Then again…' said Carlisle, who noticed the rather stupid glance upwards.

'Look, I'm innocent. Honest. Yeah, I can't say any of them are my favourite people, but I don't want them dead or anything. I've moved on. I've got my hobby.'

'Magic is your hobby?' said Carlisle.

'Yeah. Turns out my great, great, great, great grandfather had a touch of the Uncanny. It took years of practice and effort, but I've finally been able to tap into it myself. Gives me something to do, you know?'

'It's not him, is it?' said Rita, dropping into one of the other chairs in the front row.

'It's definitely not him,' replied Carlisle, 'the man's a buffoon.'

'I told you! Wait, what did you call me?'

Rita sat up straight as her skin began to crawl. 'What's that? What's happening?'

Carlisle sighed as the air around them began to ripple and haze.

'Looks like our friend here sent out a distress call.'

'So he's what, called the police on us?'

'In a way.'

The theatre melted away, to be replaced by the inside of a cave. There were no windows, no tunnels in or out, no entrances or exits of any kind.

Stood around the edge were about twenty figures. Some wore robes with magical runes and incantations stitched into the fabric with silver thread that glowed white-hot. Some wore smart, anachronistic suits. Others sported chinos and casual shirts. All in all, it was quite an odd collection of people.

Mister Nolan stood, no longer tied to a chair, as the chair didn't exist in this space.

'You could brighten the place up a little,' said Carlisle. 'A few pictures for the walls, a sofa or two, make it a bit more homely.'

'You attacked one of our own,' said one of the gathered circle of men, and they were all men, Rita noticed. Clearly this was a bit of a boys' club.

'Actually, he attacked us, and by the way...' she pulled out her badge again and showed it around the circle, 'you just abducted a police officer.'

'A hexed police officer,' replied a second member of the circle, who had a piece of gold cloth covering his face.

'So what are you lot?' asked Rita. 'Some sort of magical police?'

'Pfft,' replied Carlisle. 'This is nothing more than a wizard social club. No doubt they get together, drink, tell

Hexed Detective

tales, and attempt to impress each other with their latest tricks.'

'We also have karaoke nights,' said Mister Nolan.

'My apologies,' replied Carlisle, bowing slightly.

'She has the axe!' said one member of the circle, pointing to the handle poking out of Rita's coat.

A burble went up as they all pointed and whispered to each other.

'She has *my* axe,' Carlisle corrected, 'and if any one of you party entertainers continues to make eyes at it, you may well find them plucked out and fed to a rat.'

'Look, can I just ask if we're in any danger?' asked Rita. 'I'd like to know if I can unclench or not.'

'You can… unclench,' replied Carlisle with a look of distaste washing over his pale face.

'Great. You know, all this being in constant danger is doing wonders for my glutes.'

'Question,' said Carlisle, turning to the circle, 'a magician is murdering women in this area and you have done nothing to prevent it. Why?'

The circle shuffled their feet and avoided looking at Carlisle.

'Boys' club, isn't it? Freemasons. Illuminati. Protecting their own, right?' said Rita.

Carlisle approached one of the magicians and peered into his eyes. 'You don't know, do you? None of you?'

'He's not one of us,' replied a man with a long pointed beard that reached down to his navel. 'All local wizards and magicians are known to us.'

'We reached out to the rest of the Uncanny Kingdom's magicians,' continued another, whose idea of "magician" seemed to be, "Errol Flynn attending a film premiere in the 1930s". 'We reached out to L'Merrier, even, but no one knows who it is. Who it could be. It's a stranger.'

'Is there not some sort of magic you can do to spot him?' asked Rita. 'Izzy, wizzy, show me who he izzy. That sort of thing?'

'Yes,' replied Long Beard, 'but it doesn't work. Not on this magician. He's either beyond anything we've ever encountered, or he's being protected by something with immense power.'

'So what you're saying is, you're no help at all,' said Carlisle.

More foot shuffling.

'Well, we tried our best. Not our fault,' said Errol Flynn.

'Goodbye.' Carlisle clapped his hands together and the cave and its occupants folded back and back until the three of them, Carlisle, Rita, and Mister Nolan, were back on Blackpool's North Pier, stood outside the theatre as people bustled by, seeming not to notice the trio who had just appeared from nowhere.

'So what now?' asked Rita.

'Um, can I go home, please?' asked Mister Nolan.

Carlisle dismissed him with a wave of his hand, and the former teacher scurried away down the pier.

'Damn,' said Carlisle, walking to the edge of the pier and leaning against the barrier, his jet-black hair whipping in the sea breeze.

'What is it? What's wrong now?' asked Rita, joining him.

'It seems our options have narrowed, and I shall have to do something I really have no wish to do.'

Rita watched a pair of seagulls whirling in the sky above them.

'Sometimes I envy birds,' said Rita.

'What?'

'They can go wherever they want. Just flap off, no responsibility, no murder cases to weigh on their conscience. Just fish, the air, and a good old flap.'

'You are a very stupid person,' said Carlisle.

'I like you too, Creepy. So what is this crap thing you're going to have to do?'

Carlisle turned his back on the sea and thrust his hands deep into the pockets of his dark purple coat, his face creased with concern. Rita hadn't seen him look so worried, and it made her feel uneasy.

'What? Tell me.'

'I believe I will pay a visit to Mr. Cotton and Mr. Spike and ask them a question.'

'What? Are you insane?'

'Yes, often.'

'Won't they try to kill you?'

'Very likely, which is why I'm not trembling with giddy excitement at the prospect of knocking upon their door. But alas, I see no other move to make. Nobody seems to know anything about the person we are chasing, but we know that frightful pair do.'

Carlisle reached inside his coat and pulled out a small terracotta-coloured rectangle. It was the size and shape of a domino, and had swirling symbols scratched on to its surface.

'Here,' he said, offering it to Rita.

'What is it?'

'Insurance,' he replied.

Rita took the small tablet. It was rough to the touch, and was much weightier than its small, thin size would suggest.

'What do you mean by "insurance" exactly?'

'If things go badly, if I need pulling out, it will let you know, and it will take you to me. Do not lose it. My life, quite literally, depends upon it.' Carlisle turned, his coat sweeping, and strode away along the pier.

'What am I supposed to do in the meantime?'

Carlisle did not reply.

'Oh, nice. Well, if this thing does start glowing maybe I'll just ignore it, how do you like them, you know, bananas?... Apples! Shit.'

Rita watched Carlisle step off the pier and disappear into the hustle of the street as she rolled the terracotta domino over and over in her fingers.

Carlisle was wandering the streets of Blackpool with a destination in mind, but no direction to follow. But that was okay. He knew that sooner or later he'd end up standing in front of the door to their house.

It was fair to say that Carlisle was annoyed. Annoyed that his efforts to reclaim what was his had so far been frustrated. Annoyed that he couldn't just brush the detective aside and take his axe. Reclaim his throne. Annoyed that—of course— the case that could lead him to reclaim it had to be so complex and have such heavy hitters on the opposing side.

Heavy hitters like Mr. Cotton and Mr. Spike, and whoever this mysterious magician was. A magician whose power seemed to outreach his own. But then, Carlisle was rarely more dangerous than when on the back foot.

But still. He was annoyed. Here he was, voluntarily walking into guaranteed harm's way, having to trust that when the worst happened, a woman who barely knew a sniff of the Uncanny world would come to his aid. It made him not just annoyed, but nervous. Carlisle was never nervous.

He pulled an apple from his coat pocket and took a bite.

He'd had no direct altercations with Mr. Cotton and Mr. Spike, but knew well of their work. Of their abilities. Of the terror they could arouse in a person's mind. They could kill you, if you were lucky, or they could set up home in your head, forever. An endless nightmare.

After he had wandered aimlessly for long enough, Carlisle began to leave threads around him. Mental threads, from street to street.

'It's true, they were brothers, despite their obvious differences...' said Carlisle, imbuing each word with a call, a lure to catch the eye.

'...Mr. Cotton and Mr. Spike.'

He turned into a blind alley that hid a row of shops that had existed unseen by normal society for hundreds of years. A butcher whose window was full of meat that came from animals that were long since extinct. A shop that sold bottles of wine so intoxicating that they could slow time and warp reality around you. An antique establishment where, if you were to venture into one darkened corner, push aside a centuries-old rug, and fight through the cloud of dust that erupted from it, you'd find the now blunt head of the spear of destiny.

'They lived in a house that did not exist...'

Carlisle exited the hidden street and entered a fish and chip shop, the smell of fried cod and batter swirling around him. He walked through and to the back, pushing open the fire escape and stepping into the alley beyond.

'...And if you were to take a wrong turn one strange day,' said Carlisle, the words sparking and throbbing as they drifted around him, 'only to find yourself knocking upon this impossible home's door…'

Carlisle paused and closed his eyes. He was trembling slightly. He took a deep breath, then two, and brought himself under control. They would not see him shake. He was Carlisle, he was the one others feared. Life was a game and he was always three moves ahead.

He smiled.

'...You would soon discover that there are many worse things in this world than being lost.'

He opened his eyes to see that Blackpool was no more. Behind him was a dusty road, rolling hills covered in sparse grasses, the sky a sepia wash. He turned back to the large, lone dilapidated house before him. The brickwork was crumbled and cracked, the glass in the windows impossible to see through, with jagged shatter-lines twisting this way and that. Vegetation hugged the building tightly as if it intended to pull the entire dwelling below ground.

He had arrived.

Wherever this was. Wherever they lived. He had arrived.

He didn't bother knocking, or trying to sneak in to take them by surprise. He'd called to them and they'd let him in. They were expecting him.

Carlisle turned the door handle and pushed it open, the hinges emitting a horror movie scream.

'Nice touch,' he said loudly. His voice sounded even, strong, threaded with just a tinge of mockery. He wasn't afraid. He wasn't outmatched. He was Carlisle, and he was here for a friendly chat.

It was dark inside the house. The sort of dark that seemed alive. That seemed to press and squeeze Carlisle as he made his way, step by step, across the faded carpet, each footfall greeted by a cloud of dust.

'I like what you haven't done with the place,' said Carlisle. 'Shabby chic taken to the extreme.'

Mould crept across every surface. Carlisle wondered if the house itself was more of a vile sprouting fungus than a real bricks and mortar dwelling.

'Welcome,' said Mr. Cotton, stepping into view. He did not walk from a room, or down the stairs, it was more like he simply stepped into reality from wherever he had been lurking.

Carlisle bowed slightly. 'We meet at last,' he said, and began to wander as nonchalantly as he could around the entrance hall, peering at the age-encrusted oil paintings that adorned the walls. 'Big fan of your work, by the way. Always nice to see someone at the top of their game.'

'You flatter my brother and I, Carlisle.'

'Oh, piffle. What's true is true.'

'Mr. Spike, brother of mine, has had a particular fondness for your antics over the centuries. I've wondered often when our paths would cross.'

'And here we are at last. Face-to-face, or face-to-mask, at least.'

The rabbit mask Mr. Cotton wore grinned at that, though of course it did not, as it was just a mask.

'By the way, where is that brother of yours?'

Mr. Spike stepped out of the dark and struck Carlisle across the back of the head with the fireplace poker gripped in his white-gloved hands. Mr. Spike, his breath noisy and excited against the inside of his hedgehog mask, stood over Carlisle's unconscious body. He raised the poker a second time and looked to his brother.

'No, no,' said Mr. Cotton to his disappointed brother, 'we have things to discuss.'

Mr. Spike threw the poker aside petulantly.

'Do not despair, brother of mine. When all is said and done, you will show him your true face, and all shall be screams.'

Mr. Spike clapped his gloved hands together gleefully.

20

It had been hours since Carlisle left her behind on the pier, and Rita was starting to get worried.

She removed the terracotta domino from her pocket for the millionth time and rolled it around in her hand, traced the shape etched into it with her fingers, even held the thing to her ear in case it was supposed to make a sound. But no. She hoped that, at least, was a good thing. She also wished the lanky, pasty git had told her exactly what his plan of action was, and what she was meant to do with the thing he'd given her.

Rita huffed, shoved the piece back into her pocket, and looked towards the main entrance to Blackpool Hospital. With nothing else to do, she'd decided to pay a visit to Gemma Wheeler, the cousin of Rita's sometimes night-time partner, and prospective victim number three of the magician.

She stepped into the reception area and waved at the woman manning the desk, 'Hey there, you! It's me again, Miss Invisible, don't mind me, I'm just gonna go and check

Hexed Detective

on Gemma. Is that all right? Completely ignore me if that's all right.'

The receptionist continued to chew on the end of her pen as she read from her gossip magazine.

'Brilliant, thanks,' said Rita, and headed, unseen, behind the desk, put Gemma's name into the system, found which room she was in, and went to find her.

It was weird how quickly she'd got used to being a ghost. To being neither seen, nor heard. To not even being noticed if she physically shoved someone. She hadn't felt a thing when she'd been hexed. As she'd found herself stumbling into that secret room where Gemma Wheeler was being held, about to be sacrificed using the very axe that now swung from her belt, tapping against her right thigh as she prowled the harshly-lit corridors, avoiding oncoming orderlies.

Rita had taken it all in her stride, or at least pretended to. If she could just stay focused on the case, she wouldn't have to think about the craziness she'd fallen into. That had stolen her life from her. That had robbed her of the one chance she had to escape Blackpool, and her past. Concentrating on her job had always been Rita's way of ignoring her feelings. That and alcohol. When she needed to push down the tears and the loneliness of her childhood years, especially. That feeling of being unloved. A thing that nobody wanted to call their own.

Rita shook it off. Just think about the case, she told herself. That's all that matters. Find the killer, stop the killer.

Carlisle had assured her that Gemma would be safe. That the magician required the axe to carry out his sacrifice, and would not kill her without it, but still, Rita felt that they were being a little free and easy with the poor woman's life.

She found the room Gemma Wheeler was in. A uniformed officer was sat on a chair outside, scrolling through Twitter on his phone. Rita recognised him as Geoff

Kinney, an officer she'd once seen drink whiskey out of his own shoe.

'Just popping in to say *hey* and *how'd you do* to the almost-victim, Kinney,' said Rita.

The officer ignored her as she opened the door and stepped inside to find Gemma sat up in bed. Her erstwhile partner, Waterson, poured her a glass of water from a fat-bottomed jug.

'Oh, hi!' said Gemma, looking at Rita.

Waterson turned to see who Gemma was greeting, only, of course, to see that it was still just the two of them in the room. 'Yeah, hi,' he replied to Gemma, a little confused.

Rita waved her hands at Gemma then placed a finger to her lips. 'Shh! He can't see me,' she said.

Gemma pulled a face. 'What do you mean?'

'I mean, well, "hi", just that,' replied Waterson.

'Are you having a laugh or something? Can you not—'

Gemma's sentence was cut off as Rita placed a hand over her mouth. Waterson saw the woman pulling the strangest of faces, her lips all mushed.

'Um, here you go,' he said, handing her the glass of water. 'I'm just going to pop out and make a call, then I'll be back to go over things one more time. Is that okay?'

'Just say yeah,' said Rita, then removed her hand from Gemma's mouth.

'Just say yeah,' repeated Gemma.

'Right. Good.' Waterson took another curious look at Gemma, shook his head, and left the room.

'Okay, what the bloody hell is going on?' asked Gemma.

'You can see me?' asked Rita. 'Like, actually see me?'

'Uh, yeah, I can see you.'

'And hear me?'

'Yeah, I have ears. Why couldn't he tell you were in here?'

Rita sat on the chair that Waterson had vacated and began toying with the terracotta domino in her pocket. 'Bit hard to explain. It's also complete nonsense. If you tried to tell me similar this time last week, I'd have said you were a bloody lunatic, but you saw it. Or rather, you just saw him not seeing me, right?'

Gemma nodded slowly. 'Yeah. And?'

'How much do you remember about what happened to you? About how you got here?'

Gemma shrank. 'There was... two men. In masks.'

'From your nightmares, right?'

Gemma nodded. 'And then it's all, sort of, wispy. Not sure. I remember the arcade down on the front. I think I was taken somewhere in the back.'

'I found you, rescued you, and brought you here.'

'Oh. Cheers for that.'

'You were going to be murdered. Sacrificed. For reasons that, well, aren't entirely clear, but we're working on it.'

Gemma sipped her water. 'Okay, but that doesn't explain why he couldn't see or hear you.'

Rita wrestled with a way to explain things, then realised there was no best way, so just launched into it. 'Okay, so it turns out that when I found you I was hexed.'

'Hexed?'

'Hexed.'

'You've been hexed?'

'Completely hexed, yeah.'

'Right.' Gemma nodded as she mulled the information over. 'So what's that exactly then?'

'Hexed?'

'Yeah, what's a hex when it's at home?'

'Magic. A sort of magic curse thing.'

Rita noticed the *oh-Christ-I'm-talking-to-a-loony* look spreading across Gemma's face. 'I know, I know, it's mental, but it's true. I mean, how else do you explain me being invisible to people?'

'That maybe I'm suffering from some sort of trauma and I'm seeing things that aren't there?'

'Okay, fair answer, but I'm telling you the truth, honestly.' Rita reached out and pinched Gemma's arm.

'Oi, you bitch!' Gemma rubbed the red mark on her arm.

'See? That hurt. If I wasn't really here then I wouldn't be able to pinch you, and you wouldn't be feeling pain right now. You see my point?'

Gemma scowled as she continued to rub her arm. 'Fine. Okay. You're really here. But magic? Like David Blaine?'

'No, real, actual magic. I've seen it, and not just what's happened to me. I've seen some crazy stuff. Ooh, even a vampire in a bowling alley.'

'Fuck off.'

'Swear to God.'

'Bloody hell. Well, how come can I see you and no one else can?'

Rita shrugged. 'Buggered if I know. Maybe because you're part of all this, too? Touched with the Uncanny stuff. Oh, did you know your old teacher, Mister Nolan, can do magic now?'

'Pervy Nolan is a magician? No way!'

'It's true. We thought he might have been behind it, like he had a grudge against you all for getting him fired, but he's innocent.'

Gemma bit her lip and toyed with the edge of her blanket.

'What's wrong?' asked Rita.

'I'm scared still, you know? What if they come back for me? Rabbit Mask and his brother?'

Rita reached over and took her hand. 'It's gonna be okay. Promise.'

'How do you know, though?'

Rita opened her coat to show Gemma the axe. 'For whatever reason, they need this to carry out the sacrifice, otherwise it's pointless. And guess what?'

'What?'

'They're getting this back over my dead body.'

Rita touched the terracotta domino in her pocket and wondered how much longer Carlisle would be.

Carlisle was in a lot of trouble.

He'd regained consciousness several minutes before but had kept his eyes closed and remained motionless. He needed to think. He needed to assess the situation before Cotton and Spike realised the game was back on.

He was tied to something. Tightly. He could feel rope cutting into his wrists, his ankles, his throat. The rope around his throat made it difficult to breathe—constricting his windpipe to half its usual diameter—but he did not panic. He continued to breathe slow and steady. All would be fine. He just needed to find the right things to say. He'd talked his way out of worse. Far worse.

Actually, that wasn't true, but he lied to others successfully on such a regular basis that he hoped to be able to fool himself, too.

He could not.

'How much longer will you go on pretending?' came a voice. Mr. Cotton.

'I take it the jig is up,' replied Carlisle, opening one eye to see Mr. Cotton sat in a brown leather chair, legs crossed, a couple of metres in front of him.

'You cannot fool us here, Carlisle. Nobody can. Not even as adept a liar as yourself.'

'Well, that hardly seems fair.'

'Oh, life isn't fair. Never has been. And nightmares? Nightmares are made from unfair. And fear. And pain. They are delicious.'

Mr. Cotton's mouth opened and a velvet tongue wormed out to lick his lips. Only of course it did not, as the mask was just a mask, and that was impossible.

Carlisle opened both eyes and swallowed, painfully. He was roped to a chair. He began to test the ropes, hoping to slowly create some wiggle room. Some give. Some hope of escape. The ropes offered no hope at all.

'Why am I restrained?' asked Carlisle. 'Surely you have no need to incapacitate me. No need to fear.'

'We do not fear, my brother and I.' Mr. Cotton stood and held out a gloved hand. A second gloved hand reached out of the dark, out of the nothing, and took hold: Mr. Spike stepping out of the shadows to join them.

'You know, hitting a man from behind is not very gentlemanly behaviour, Mr. Spike,' said Carlisle.

Mr. Spike's shoulders shook and he made a wet, wheezing noise that might have been laughter.

'Why have you paid us a visit, Carlisle?' asked Mr. Cotton.

'I have a question for you.'

'Oh? A question worth dying for?'

'Nothing is worth dying for.'

Mr. Cotton and Mr. Spike began to waltz together around the room.

'You do not usually help others, Carlisle,' said Mr. Cotton.

'I don't care about the detective,' he replied. 'I care only for what is mine.'

'Not yours. Not anymore. It is needed.'

Carlisle strained at the ropes, sweat running down his forehead and into his eyes. Just a little give. That's all he needed.

Mr. Cotton and his brother stopped dancing and turned to face Carlisle.

'See how he strains and struggles, brother?'

Mr. Spike nodded, shoulders shaking as a giant centipede crawled from one of his mask's eyeholes.

'He has lived for so very long, and yet he demands more regardless of the hopelessness of his situation. Tell me, Carlisle, do you ever have nightmares?'

'I do not sleep, nor do I dream.'

'Oh, you will find that you do not require sleep to experience nightmares,' said Mr. Cotton, and his long ears twitched, but of course they did not. 'You had a question for us?'

Carlisle paused in his pointless struggle against the ropes, which seemed only to wind tighter the more he fought. He blinked his eyes clear. 'Who is your employer?'

'Ah. Now that is the question, isn't it? Who is the great and powerful Oz?'

'Tell me.'

Mr. Cotton stepped towards him, taking Carlisle's chin in his gloved hand and tilting his head up.

'Pray, have you heard tell of the Angel of Blackpool?'

Carlisle knew the story. He'd heard it whispered once, centuries before. 'It is a fantasy. A fairy tale.'

Mr. Cotton wagged a gloved finger in front of Carlisle's face. 'No, no, no. It has always been true.'

'Okay. So the Magician is this Angel?'

Mr. Spike wheezed his horrid laugh again.

'I see. Then the Magician is just working for the Angel, like the two of you? Thanks for the information.'

'Oh, is he not a blabbermouth, my brother?' said Mr. Cotton, patting Mr. Spike on the shoulder and dislodging a whorl of brown dust.

'What is the harm?' asked Carlisle. 'I shall never leave here alive.'

'Never has a truer statement been uttered, Your Majesty.'

'So?'

Mr. Cotton looked at him with his blank, stationary face for several seconds.

The only sound in the room came from Mr. Spike's heavy, rasping breath. He nodded his head slightly. 'The Angel of Blackpool will rise with our assistance.'

'And the Magician's,' replied Carlisle.

'Of course.'

'Why?'

'No, no. Too much.'

'Okay, then why do you help? What is your price?'

'We enjoy our work, my brother and I, but we are restrained from reaching our true, beautiful potential. We have been promised that these restraints will be removed. The world shall become one endless nightmare, and we shall feast, and we shall dance, and we shall frolic until our hearts burst with glee.'

Mr. Spike clapped his hands together excitedly.

A clock bonged in the distance and Mr. Cotton pulled out a pocket watch to check the time.

'Well, well. It seems that time has rather run away with us, and your visit is at an end.'

'But I have more questions,' said Carlisle.

'Brother, mine.'

Mr. Spike nodded and began to step towards Carlisle. He did not walk, he swayed, hands behind his back, each footstep a delicate, dancer's sweep.

'Maybe we can help each other out; form a beneficial

understanding,' said Carlisle. 'All I want, at the end of this, is what's mine.'

'Hear how he attempts to curry favour, to cut deals, to stab associates who trust him so, directly in the back. Tut tut, sir. Very bad form.'

'I can help you. Ask your Angel.'

'Thank you for paying our humble home a visit, we get so few willing visitors,' said Mr. Cotton. 'This has been a rare treat, especially to play host to such a distinguished, cruel, nefarious guest as your good self.'

Carlisle struggled and strained, rocking the chair back and forth until it tumbled to one side. His head bounced off the carpeted floor.

'Wriggle, please do,' said Mr. Cotton. 'It makes this all the more delicious.'

Carlisle was beyond pretence now. Beyond saving face. Beyond dignity. He screamed and he shouted and he tried to close his eyes, even though they refused to do as he wished. It was no use. He was lost.

Mr. Spike crouched before him, cocking his head to one side, rancid air wheezing from behind the mask, dampening Carlisle's face with his putrid breath.

'Shall he show you true horror?' asked Mr. Cotton.

Carlisle did not answer. His body relaxed. He accepted his fate. To struggle any more was pointless.

'Brother, mine,' said Mr. Cotton.

And then Mr. Spike removed his mask, and Carlisle saw the face beneath.

And the world became screams and terror.

21

Rita pulled her coat tight as she looked up at the darkening sky, her breath forming like dragon smoke in the frigid air.

She'd spent another hour talking with Gemma Wheeler, but eventually left her to it with promises made that the case would soon be done, and that she'd be able to return home, safe.

Rita even mostly believed it.

'Carlisle, where the shit are you?' she muttered.

He'd been gone close to four hours, and she was starting to wonder if she was ever going to see him again. Maybe he'd decided to bail on the case. Forget about the axe he claimed was his. It's not as though she had any good reason to trust him. Formby, that moley-looking old man, had said as much to her. Carlisle was a liar. A dangerous cheat. And yet she was relying on him to help save Gemma Wheeler's life. To save her own life, too. Okay, her everyday life might have been slowly suffocating her, but it was a heck of a lot better than her current situation, living in limbo land, a human ghost.

Before Rita left the hospital, Waterson had briefly re-entered Gemma Wheeler's room to give her assurances that he was on the case. Rita would have given just about anything for him to have turned to her at that point, to have seen her, and delivered one of his usual withering remarks. Her partner—her best friend for years—and he didn't even remember her.

That stung. She hadn't just been made to disappear, her very existence, her history, had been scrubbed out. She wasn't even a memory anymore.

Rita swore and rubbed at her eyes as she felt them growing damp and heavy. 'Pull yourself together, you daft tart.'

Detective.

Rita winced and clutched her temples as the voice, with that single word, seemed to burn inside her head.

Detective, find me.

'Carlisle?' Rita stood and looked around, but he was nowhere to be seen. He hadn't spoken to her, she hadn't heard his voice, she'd *felt* it.

Reaching into her coat, she yanked out the terracotta domino and stared at it in wonder. The shapes, the squiggles and scratches, now burned a brilliant white. Carlisle was calling to her.

'Hello?' she said to the thing, then placed it to her ear as though it were a phone. 'Carlisle, where are you? Can you hear me?'

There was no answer, but the domino continued to glow, and now it seemed to pulse in her palm as though it had a heartbeat.

'Shit. How do I use this thing? I don't understand what I'm supposed to do, you lanky goon.'

And then the world bulged and stretched and warped, and a rip opened in the fabric of reality.

'Oh,' said Rita.

Peering through the impossible tear, she could see what looked like a room in an old house. She looked back to the hospital's entrance, down at the glowing terracotta domino, then through to the room beyond the tear.

'Okay, well. Looks like I'm doing something dumb again.'

Rita pulled the axe from her belt, held out her domino-holding hand, and edged through the tear. It wasn't like she'd stepped through a rip in the world, it was as though she'd stepped from one room into another. No big deal.

She turned to see the rip in reality was still open. She could see a man in a dressing gown leaning against the hospital's wall, smoking a cigarette. She wondered how long it would stay open.

The domino pulsed rapidly in her hand as if trying to get her mind back on the job, which, she assumed, was finding Carlisle. If that meant he was in trouble, that he needed saving, then what chance did she have? He knew this world inside out, he was part of it. He was clearly powerful in ways he wasn't willing to share, so if he was trapped, what would happen to her; a Blackpool copper with a magic hatchet?

She looked around the room she'd found herself in. It was, in a word, creepy. Or in three words: "creepy as fuck". It was an old-fashioned bedroom for a child; piles of toys strewn around the floor, a small cot in one corner, a mobile hanging above it. It looked to Rita as though it belonged in some ancient Victorian house, the kind you see in period dramas on the telly, only this one had been left to go... rotten. Everything was faded, warped, degraded. Mould crept across almost every surface, and it seemed to Rita that unseen things watched her from the room's darkened corners.

She gripped the axe tightly and made her way towards the closed bedroom door. She turned the brass handle and the door opened with a sharp cry that made Rita gasp. She stopped and counted to ten, listening for any movement outside of the room, for any sign that the door had alerted someone in a rabbit or hedgehog mask that they had an unwanted guest.

All was silent.

Trying to control her breathing, Rita spoke to herself. 'Be brave, Detective.'

A man, if he was even a man, was in trouble, and this was her job. Protect. Take down the bad guys. No time for fear when duty called.

'Bad-ass. Bad-ass bitch.' Rita nodded and slipped out of the open door into the corridor beyond.

It was, like the child's bedroom she'd entered through, brown and rotten. It was lined with paintings of figures in grand frames. Each painting depicted one or both of Mr. Cotton and Mr. Spike.

Carlisle had said the pair were literally the stuff of nightmares, and if the stuff of nightmares lived anywhere, it would be a house like this.

Rita began to edge along the corridor, half-expecting the eyes in the paintings to follow her. For a hand to reach out of one of them and grip her shoulder with a dirty white glove.

Each footfall was greeted by the complaint of a rotten floorboard, and the corridor seemed to twist and sway as she made her way along it.

'How do I know where you are?' Rita whispered into the still-pulsating domino, its carved shapes blazing brilliantly.

She tried the first door she passed. It opened into another bedroom, though this one was not empty. Hundreds of tiny yellow eyes turned to regard her, every inch of the room swamped with large black rats, their rotten teeth chattering.

'Sorry, wrong room,' said Rita, and made sure the door was very firmly closed as she hurried away.

At the end of the corridor was a rather grand staircase leading down to the ground floor.

'Carlisle?' she said, her voice a hiss, but there was no response. 'Carlisle, if you're close, make this domino throb hard twice.'

It did not throb hard twice.

Rita made her way down the staircase. The house stank of decay, and the air was thick with dust, making it hard to breathe. At the bottom of the stairs, Rita took a right, only for the domino to stop pulsing.

'Okay, hot or cold?' She turned left, instead, and took a few steps, and the thing began its heartbeat pulse once again. 'Right, hot.'

She stopped in front of a door, waving the domino in front of it. It shone so brightly she couldn't look at it.

'Bingo.'

Rita opened the door. Inside, was a grand ballroom, far too large for what the house could realistically contain. A giant chandelier hung from the vaulted ceiling, every crystal contained within it cracked, or broken in two, or missing entirely. Long tables with yellowed table cloths crowded the room. Thick grey cobwebs were strung from one silver candelabra to the next, and spiders lazily roamed the piles of rotten food, picking up fat flies that gorged on the oozing, rotten mess.

The stench was like a punch to the face, and it took everything Rita had not to stumble out of the room and vomit. She'd have liked to have done that, but something else was in the room. *Someone* else.

Carlisle.

He was laid on his side on the floor, roped to a chair. Blood was soaked into the dirty carpet in a halo around his head, and dried tributaries of red ran from his mouth, his nose, his ears, even his eyes.

Hexed Detective

'Carlisle!' She ran to him, kneeling, patting his face. 'Hey, I'm here. Your thingy worked. Wake up.'

She hit him harder, shook him. He didn't wake, didn't make a sound. Didn't even twitch.

'Shit, shit, shit,' said Rita, feeling for a pulse.

No pulse.

Did he ever have a pulse? He must have done. And then something sparked in Rita's mind and she looked down at the terracotta domino in her hand, slowly pulsing away, one heartbeat after another.

'You've got to be kidding me…'

It had only started to glow, to pulse, when he needed help. Rita was starting to put two and two together when something tapped against her foot. She looked down to a rat staring up at her, sat back on its hind legs, its front paws rubbing together.

'Sod off,' she said, and kicked the squealing rodent across the room.

Pocketing the domino, Rita hacked at the ropes binding Carlisle, and freed his body—his corpse?—from the chair.

'Carlisle, mate, you're going to have to help me out here.'

He had always looked alabaster white, as pale as a ghost, but now his skin looked grey.

'How did you get here?' came a voice.

Rita spun round, but there was nobody there. She brandished the axe warily.

'Oi, who's there then, hey?'

A floorboard squeaked in a shadowed corner. Rita turned and swung the axe impotently.

'Stop messing around, okay? You don't scare me, I've faced worse on the job.'

Worse than some nightmare monster who lurked in a house built from fear and rot who could apparently kill

Carlisle with little effort? Yeah, she may have been bluffing just a little there.

'I asked you a question,' said the voice.

Rita turned again to see the carpet in one corner of the room ripple and bulge. The carpet tore and up sprouted a pair of rabbit ears.

'Shit!' Rita grabbed Carlisle, sitting him up. 'Come on, you dead idiot, we've gotta move.'

'They always run and run and run but there's never anywhere to go.'

With a cry, Rita managed to lever the chair holding Carlisle back into an upright position.

Mr. Cotton rose fully into the room, a rat on his shoulder. 'You kicked Reginald. Reginald is not happy.' The rat squeaked furiously at Rita, then hopped down into Mr. Cotton's gloved hand. 'Sleepy time, Reginald.' The rabbit mask's mouth stretched wide into a Edvard Munch scream, and Reginald the oily, fat-tailed rat hopped inside. The mouth closed behind him.

The exit, the tear Rita had stepped into this house from, that she could still hopefully escape through, was all the way upstairs. There was no way she'd make it, at least not carrying Carlisle's dead weight. That's if the thing was still even open. Nope, Rita was pretty much screwed.

Deciding she had no intention of going out on the back foot, Rita took a step forward and shook the axe at Mr. Cotton. 'Stay back, all right, or I'll twat you with this thing, you murdering, weird, bastarding bastard.'

'Oh, Reginald is not dead. I would never kill a rat.'

'I'm talking about Carlisle.'

Mr. Cotton's masked head tilted. 'Oh, yes. That was fun. So brave to come here. In the end he screamed, though. Screamed as my brother showed him true terror and his

Hexed Detective

brain hubbled and bubbled and turned to naught but mush. A skull full of mashed potato.'

A gurgling, hacking sound alerted Rita to the fact that Mr. Spike had joined them. She swung around to see him stood behind her, shoulders juddering as the awful noise dribbled and rattled from beneath his hedgehog mask.

'Oh, that's funny is it?' asked Rita.

'My brother, Mr. Spike, does enjoy the lighter side of life, it is true. And now, the axe. I believe you shall give it to me so the work can resume, yes?'

Mr. Cotton reached out with one hand and began to move calmly towards Rita.

'Yeah, not bloody likely, you big freak,' she stepped back, swinging the axe to ward Mr. Cotton off, but Mr. Cotton did not pause.

'For shame. Such rude manners for one so fair,' he said.

Rita, heart smashing against her chest, looked back to see Mr. Spike guarding the door as his brother continued to advance.

'Stay back!' Rita demanded, swinging again.

'No, no, and no again. The axe is ours and nothing but nightmares upon nightmares shall be yours. I will show you everything that makes you shout and scream, over and over, and then my brother will show you what lurks beneath his mask. It will be delicious,' said Mr. Cotton, as Reginald the rat poked his snout out of one of the rabbit mask's eye holes and chittered his yellow, broken teeth.

No way back without stumbling into Mr. Spike, and Mr. Cotton was almost upon her. Rita was out of options. She took a breath, stepped forward, and, with a war cry, swung the axe, missing Mr. Cotton completely and sending her tumbling to the floor.

'Tut-tut,' said Mr. Cotton. 'A swing and a miss.' He clicked his thumb and forefinger together and a tentacle burst from the rotten food piled upon the table. It wrapped itself around Rita's leg and began to drag her across the floor.

'Let me go!' she yelled.

'Don't you know better than to play with your food?' said Mr. Cotton, and Mr. Spike gurgle-laughed once more.

Rita rolled on to her back to see what she was being dragged towards, the rotten food now a writhing alive thing. The spiders that crawled upon it were growing, and growing, their twitching, fang-like mouthparts dripping with blood. Rita was terrified, but even in her terror, realised that this was what Mr. Cotton wanted. He wanted her fear.

'What dreadful delights we shall show to you, what scares we shall conjure.'

'Up yours!' screamed Rita, and swung the axe at the tentacle, severing it.

The rotten food bucked and screamed, the tentacle thrashing, spraying the room with viscous black blood.

'Naughty,' said Mr. Cotton. 'You shall be punished.'

But Rita wasn't listening. As she struck the tentacle, she did not just sever the limb that was pulling her towards an horrific death. No, she connected to the magic. To the nightmare power of Mr. Cotton, of Mr. Spike, of their horror house. She felt it coursing through the axe. It was just like with Mister Nolan, the gropey ex-teacher. The axe had connected to something Uncanny and was giving Rita access to its magic. Letting her understand it. Sense it. Control it.

She raised the axe in wonder, its head raging with sorcery, black and purple and deep red coiling around and through.

Mr. Cotton was rushing towards her, but she had nothing to fear. She felt the dark magic embolden her as she turned from him and struck out at the tables, at the rotting food, and made a demand.

Tentacles burst from the gross mass and rushed at Mr. Cotton, gripping his ankles, his wrists, his neck.

'You are a very bad house guest,' said Mr. Cotton, and then the tentacles tore him into pieces and pulled the wriggling bits into the disgusting mass of food and out of sight.

'Ha!' said Rita, staring gleefully at the axe.

She turned to see Mr. Spike, his shoulders heaving, for the first time seemingly unsure of what to do.

'That's right, mate. Think twice before rushing this bad-ass bitch.'

She felt elated. She had taken Mr. Cotton by surprise, but now Mr. Spike knew what she could do, it might not be the smartest thing to rush him. No, the best course of action was to escape this place, but the portal was still all the way upstairs, and, furthermore, past Mr. Spike.

But then Mr. Cotton and Mr. Spike had control over this house. Over this dreamscape. Could create exit points. And Rita had access to that power. To instinctively understand it.

She swung the axe and buried its head in the floor, soaking up the Uncanny that made up the nightmare abode.

'Somewhere safe,' said Rita.

She looked down at the axe in her hands, to the blade that glowed fiercely, every colour imaginable strobing and coiling around it. The colours of magic.

'Somewhere safe,' she said again, and then pulled the axe head from the floor and swung it until it connected with the fabric of the nightmare place's reality, and sliced open a gap. A way out.

Senses sharp, she heard ragged, angry breaths and whirled around in time to see Mr. Spike, his hedgehog mask twisted into a furious snarl, his gloved hands reaching for her. Without thinking, the axe found its new target, sinking into Mr. Spike's head.

A sound like twisting metal erupted from Mr. Spike's mask as his body spasmed, and for a few seconds, Rita felt herself connected to his magic. Dark, horrible magic that soaked into the axe. Became part of it, ready to be unleashed.

She pulled the weapon free and Mr. Spike fell to the floor, his body exploding into a hundred screeching, writhing rats.

'Well that was… unexpected,' said Rita, as the rodents scurried in every direction but hers.

Rita threw Carlisle's lifeless arm over her shoulder and dragged him to the exit she'd created, her body crying out with pain as she bore his weight. She stumbled through the exit point in the dreamscape and fell to the floor beyond. As she collapsed to the ground, Rita rolled on to her back and found the exit point was already gone.

She'd done it.

She'd made it out.

She sagged back, the laughter of disbelief pouring out of her.

'Oh, it's you, is it? How's the case going, eh?'

Rita saw Formby, the ancient eaves, stood over her. She was back in Big Pins.

'Help me,' said Rita. 'Carlisle's dead.'

22

Waterson pulled to a stop on Blackpool's seafront and looked out at the water beyond the beach.

Watching the waves rush in and out always soothed him. Took his mind off his problems, at least as long as he just followed the water like a metronome, in and out, steady as she goes, lulling him, calming him down.

Today it wasn't working.

He got out of his car and walked closer to the water, listening to the waves washing in and out, trying to force his mind to empty itself, just for a minute or two.

No good.

Maybe it was the pressure of the job finally overwhelming him. His mum had always been worried about him going into such a dangerous career, mixing with the worst of the worst. He'd waved her off, though. He'd always known he was meant to be a copper, ever since he was five and had became obsessed with old black and white Sherlock Holmes films. The ones with Basil Rathbone.

Okay, he might not exactly be a modern day Holmes, but he was good at his job. Most of the time, anyway. And he felt good about the difference he was able to make to this place, his home town, but now…

The case was unusual for the area. Three women kidnapped, three women connected by age, by school, by… something else. *Rabbit ears*. Waterson shook his head and looked out to sea once again.

Out to sea.

Well, that hit the nail on the head. There was so much about the case that Waterson didn't understand. First, there was the mysterious rescue of the third abductee, who couldn't remember who had delivered her, unconscious, to Blackpool Hospital. An abductee who no one in the busy reception area had seen, and who wasn't picked up on a single CCTV camera. One moment Gemma Wheeler was nowhere to be seen, then a burst of static and there she was, slumped in a wheelchair. *Ta-da!* A magic trick, minus the magician. That part of the case was seriously off, and Waterson had no idea how to process it. How to account for it at all.

But then there was the other thing. The forgotten thing. The thing that churned his stomach and made the day feel like a foggy dream.

Waterson turned from the sea, frustrated, and looked over to the noise and riot of lights across the road. Archer's Old Arcade. The last place Gemma Wheeler remembered before waking up in a hospital room. Not that she remembered much, or why it was or wasn't significant. All she knew was that, at some point, she was there. She had the image of the machines, the claw games, the lights streaked across her mind's eye, like she'd rushed through, semi-conscious, her slurred memory taking an indistinct snapshot. Or perhaps it meant nothing at all. A trick of a traumatised brain.

And yet it was all he had to go on. Gemma Wheeler had given them nothing else that he could use to gain a toehold.

Waterson sighed and ran across the road towards the

Hexed Detective

arcade, skipping past oncoming traffic, an angry food delivery driver honking the horn of his moped as he swerved by him.

Officers had already been to the arcade to question staff, managers, frequent visitors, anyone who spent more time than they should hanging out in the place. They brandished pictures of Gemma Wheeler and were greeted with head-shaking and shoulder shrugs. No one had seen her in the place. That did not mean, of course, that she hadn't been there. A lot of people crowded into that arcade on a daily basis, and no one was taking in faces – they were focused on screens, on grasping claws, on penny shove machines. Easy for someone to pass in and out unnoticed.

They'd searched the place, Waterson included, and found nothing. So why was he back? Because the hairs on the back of his neck insisted he'd missed something. He liked to think he had good instincts as a cop. It was one of the things that gave him such a solid arrest record. He'd missed something. They all had. But what? And would he recognise it even if he saw it?

He weaved slowly around the floor of Archer's Old Arcade, letting his eyes drift over every person, every machine, every surface, waiting for something to leap out at him.

He stopped by a claw machine. A young girl, no older than seven or eight, long blonde hair in bunches, tongue sticking out, was studiously manoeuvring the grasping metal claw over a pile of plush toys. These things were always rigged. It was almost impossible to win. The claw never closed enough for whatever toy it grabbed to make it all the way to the exit chute.

Down went the claw and the metal fingers closed just enough to raise one of the soft toys away from the others. It cleared the rest of the toys, swung back and forth, then tumbled out of the claw's grasp. The girl stomped her foot then fed another coin into the hungry machine. Out went the claw again, the girl steering its progress with the small joystick. Left, then right, then back, then the girl smacked the red button and the claw plunged again into the abundance of toys, grasping one, pulling it up into view.

There went the hairs on the back of Waterson's neck again.

A rabbit swung precariously from the metal claw, the scarf it had around its neck snagged on one of the fingers.

Rabbit ears.

'They all had the same nightmare,' Waterson said to himself. He wasn't sure why, but as he said it, he knew it was true.

He turned from the machine, from the toy rabbit, and followed his feet. Somehow, they seemed to know where they were going.

The stockroom.

This was where he'd had that feeling the last time he was here. That sense of missing something.

The door swung shut and the sound of the arcade became muffled.

He ran his hands over the giant plastic bags stuffed full of toys. A pair of rabbit ears poked out of a hole in one of the bags. Waterson reached out and stroked them.

'What? What is it?' he said, hitting the heel of his hand against his temple, trying to dislodge a blockage he felt sure was there.

He sagged and turned to leave, but stopped as something caught his eye.

It was a door.

The door hadn't been there during his last visit to the stockroom, he was sure of it. Hadn't been there when he checked it out this time, either. But now there it was. A door.

Waterson tried the handle. Locked. He ran from the stockroom and found the manager, pulling the befuddled man behind him and into the stockroom.

'What are you talking about?' asked the manager, as he was bundled into the room, almost piled into a bag of toys.

'Do you have a key for the door?' asked Waterson.

'What door?'

'That one.' Waterson pointed at the door, the air catching in his throat.

No door.

He raced over to it and began to frantically run his hands over the brickwork.

'Hey, are you… okay?' asked the manager.

Waterson turned to him, eyes wide, and didn't know what to say.

23

Despite his advanced age, Formby had the strength of a bull.

Rita watched in surprise as, with seemingly little effort, the ancient eaves grabbed the dead weight of Carlisle and tossed him over one shoulder.

'Follow me,' he said, hurrying past the gawping faces of Big Pins' regulars and heading behind the bar.

Despite the terrible circumstances, Rita still found herself giggling at the absurd sight of this short mole-man carrying Carlisle's long, narrow corpse, the knuckles of his white, elegant hands dragging a grim trail along the carpet.

Linton, the hulking proprietor of the Uncanny gathering spot, ushered Formby and Rita to a door behind the bar.

'Dead, is he?' asked Linton. 'Shame.'

Rita followed Formby and the late Carlisle into the back room, a small, shabby office stacked high with boxes containing bar snacks and bowling shoes. Linton yanked a cord and a bare bulb spluttered to life, casting a sickly yellow glow around the faded room. Formby headed for the sole item of furniture, a shabby couch, foam bursting from rips in its upholstery, and dumped Carlisle's body unceremoniously onto it.

'He better not leak any bodily juices and what-not on my furniture,' said Linton, before leaving them to it, closing the door as he left.

'Is he dead?' asked Rita. 'He's dead, isn't he? I mean, I couldn't feel a pulse or anything, so that means he's dead, right?'

Formby prised open one of Carlisle's eyes and peered at it.

'Did he ever even have a pulse?' Rita asked. 'He looked sort of like a vampire, like from a film—not *Twilight* shit, but a good one—so maybe he didn't have a pulse anyway.' Rita realised she was pacing in a little circle and flapping her hands as she spoke, so decided to stop doing that.

'Where was he?' asked Formby, levering Carlisle's jaw open with a knife and shining a small torch down his exposed throat.

'In a house. A creepy house. The creepiest.'

'He paid Mr. Cotton and Mr. Spike a visit?' asked Formby, turning to Rita as he did, his eyes wide with surprise.

'Yeah. He said he wanted to ask them a question, about the case we're on. Wouldn't let me go with him.'

'Huh,' said Formby. 'Put himself in danger, did he? Not like him to go and do a thing like that for someone else.'

'Look, is he dead or not? Because he seems pretty dead to me.'

Formby straightened up and turned off the torch, slipping it in the inside pocket of his dirty, grey coat. 'Oh yes. Dead as a dead person, that's what he is. The spark of life has spluttered its last.'

'Oh, Jesus,' said Rita, dropping to her haunches and scraping her fingers through her thick red hair.

'Must trust you, then,' said Formby.

'What?'

'Trust you. He put his life in your hands.'

'Well, he's dead, so that looks like a bit of a mistake, doesn't it?'

Formby began to laugh. 'No, no, no. I'm talking literally. Life in your hands.'

Rita stood, feeling suddenly very tired indeed. Tired and alone on a case that had erased her from normal life, and that now, without Carlisle at her side, she saw no way of solving.

'Stop talking in riddles, mole-face. I'm knackered, I'm angry, I'm sad, and I don't mind hitting you with this axe. Okay?'

'Did he give you it?'

Rita sighed. 'Give me what?'

'His life?'

Rita was about to reply with a string of expletives when she remembered the terracotta domino with its elaborately-carved patterns. She reached into her coat pocket and pulled it out. The thing glowed, still, throbbing rhythmically.

'Oh. This is his life, isn't it?' asked Rita, holding the item close to her face, the light it cast warming her skin.

Formby nodded. 'That's right. Good bit of magic that if you've got the knowledge of it.'

'He said it was an insurance policy.'

Formby clapped his hands together then reached to her. 'Give it over, then. The longer he's dead, the more painful it'll be when he's not dead.'

Rita moved to pass the piece to Formby, then hesitated. 'Wait, how do I know I can trust you? That you're not just gonna, I dunno, snap this thing in two? It's not as though you and Carlisle are best mates.'

Formby grinned. 'You do not know you can trust me,

true. That is the world you're in now. More often than not, you trust the untrustworthy.'

'Well, that's my mind put at ease.'

Rita handed the piece to Formby, who took it gingerly between thumb and forefinger.

'Right. Right, then. I think I remember how you do this.'

Formby pulled the knife he'd used to open Carlisle's mouth back out of its sheath, raised it high above his head, then brought it down with a grunt of effort. The blade slid into Carlisle's chest like it was made of sponge, not flesh and bone.

'Jesus!' cried Rita, stepping back as Formby waggled the blade back and forth, opening a cavity in Carlisle's chest.

'There we go, feller,' he said, the glowing domino now slowly writhing back and forth like a fat slug. Formby lowered it into the gap he'd created in Carlisle's chest, then let it go. The terracotta domino wriggled its way into the hole and disappeared from view.

Then nothing happened.

'He still seems very dead to me,' noted Rita.

Formby frowned and peered at the corpse on the couch. 'Yeah, he does a bit. Wait a minute.'

Formby spat on his hand, balled it into a fist, then bashed it against Carlisle's chest like he was the Fonz jolting a jukebox into life.

Carlisle was a corpse no more.

His eyes snapped open and he sat bolt upright, gasping for air, clutching his wounded chest.

'All right, all right,' said Formby, 'don't go fussing just because you've been dead for a bit.' He guided the twitching Carlisle into a foetal position on the couch and patted him on the head.

'Carlisle?' said Rita, stepping towards him.

'No, no,' said Formby, shooing her away. 'Wait out there

a while, he'll need a bit of a sleep yet. You can't expect a man who's just been dead to be at his best right off.'

'He's alive. I mean, he was dead, now he's alive!'

'There's those keen detection skills again,' said Carlisle, his voice an arid whisper.

'Oi, you, hush,' said Formby. 'Sleep now, rudeness later.'

Rita laughed in disbelief. She'd done it. She'd saved him.

Rita thanked Linton as he placed a second pint of ale in front of her.

'You know, you could've just left him for dead,' he said.

'Yes, you've already said that,' replied Rita, as Linton frowned and made his way back to the bar, where a patron was waiting to swap his dirty boots for a pair of bowling shoes.

It had been almost an hour since Carlisle stopped being a corpse, and neither he nor Formby had emerged from the back room. Rita was itching to know what he'd found out. If he'd managed to get anything useful out of the terrifying masked pair before they'd murdered him.

She shook her head and took a gulp of her pint. A weird man had gone to a nightmare house to talk to monsters who had killed him. Only the death didn't stick because of some sort of magic nonsense. It was a wonder she hadn't gone mad yet.

She reached down and took out the axe, placing it on the table before her. It had saved her life again. It was weird, the effect it had. The way it seemed to connect her to the magic of whatever she went up against. How it seemed to make her understand it. *See* it. Know just how to wrangle it for her own needs. For as long as she needed it— for as long as she held the axe and it translated the spell—

she wasn't a stranger to this bizarre world. No, for a few brief moments, she was part of it. Connected to it. The master of it.

She stroked the blunt-looking blade with the tips of her fingers and felt a shiver of something run up her hand. Potential, that's what it was. There was magic still inside it. She'd hit both of them after all, hadn't she? Mr. Cotton and Mr. Spike. She'd used Cotton's magic to create an escape point, but Spike's magic still lurked, unused, inside of it.

Rita wrapped her hands around the handle and lifted the axe. It reacted to her touch. She felt as though the axe knew that magic dwelled within it, and was waiting for her to tell it how to use it.

'Talking to you, is it?'

Rita pulled her hands away from the axe, her concentration broken by Formby, who sat down and availed himself of her partially-drunk pint of ale.

'There's magic in it. Right now,' said Rita.

'That so?' replied Formby, smacking his lips, foam from the ale speckling his rough beard.

'I hit them with it. Both of them: Cotton and Spike. Took some of their magic and used it, somehow, to come here.'

'That's handy,' said Formby, waving his hand at the bar to catch Linton's attention. Linton nodded and began to pull two fresh drinks.

'How is he? Carlisle?'

'Oh, he's been better, I expect. Though, he's been dead before, of course.'

'He's what?'

'Got to expect it, the life he leads. Why he makes sure he has insurance when he needs it. He's not stupid. Nasty, untrustworthy, ruthless, murderous, but no, not stupid.'

Linton placed the fresh pints on the table and Formby

licked his lips, reaching out with both hands to grasp his glass.

'He's not shat himself in there, has he?' asked Linton. 'I've heard they do that, after being dead for a bit.'

'No, no, nothing wet has left his body,' replied Formby.

'Hm.' Linton turned and headed back to his bar.

'Apart from being alive, how actually is he?'

Formby frowned and considered the question. 'Tired, and weak, which is to be expected of course. Does nothing for your get-up-and-go, a bit of being dead, oh no. He's trying to put a brave face on it, but I seen it in his eyes.'

'What?'

'Well, they show you things, Mr. Cotton and Mr. Spike. Things to turn the sanest man mad. Kill you with the madness, they do. They showed Carlisle something, all right. Something that stopped his heart stone dead. I saw down his throat; red-raw from screaming in there.' Formby shivered and gulped his drink.

'But he'll be okay?'

Formby shrugged. 'Okay enough. In a while. Never quite the same, I'd imagine, but alive.'

Rita sighed with relief and sat back. She'd rescued him, saved a life, even if she wasn't entirely sure how. That's what you did in the force, you had your partner's back. She thought about all the times she'd pulled Waterson's arse out of the fire and smiled.

'Suppose it's time I told you a thing or two,' said Formby.

'Hm? Sorry, what did you say?'

'Whilst his nibs is incapacitated out back, thought you might like to hear a thing or two I've heard whispered on the wind about you,' he said flicking his pointed ears and grinning, displaying his twin set of higgledy-piggledy piranha teeth.

Rita sat forward, wrapping her hands around the handle to her axe. 'There's whispers about me?'

'Whispers and words, and here's me, an old eaves with the ear-lugs to hear it and all that knowledge safe and sound in my brain meat.'

Rita wasn't sure she liked the idea of people talking about her. People in this Uncanny world, at least. What was there to whisper about, anyway?

'Well? Go on then.'

'An eaves requires payment to share.'

'Payment?'

'Fair's fair. Got to make a living, haven't we?'

'Okay, how much?'

'A promise of magic to feast upon. You have it coming your way.'

'Right, fine, whatever, just tell me.'

Formby clapped his fingerless-gloved hands together, the nails on each digit sharp and yellow. 'Then the transaction is fair,' he said. 'I did some digging. Went to the right places. Lurked and listened. No person living had anything of worth to say, but I found a few old ghosts in Friar's Cemetery swapping stories, and up came your name.'

Rita blinked slowly as she took this in. 'I'm sorry, did you say ghosts? There are ghosts, and they're talking about me?'

Formby grinned and nodded.

'Good. Good to know. Not creepy at all, that. On you go then.'

'Carlisle wondered why his artefact, the axe, came to be yours without the wielder's consent, yes?'

'Yes.'

'It's simple, see? It is a thing of Heaven.'

'Yeah, you said that already. So what?'

'So, it is inclined to buddy up with other things of Heaven, understand?'

'Not at all, no.'

'Other things of Heaven... such as you.'

Rita nodded slowly. 'I'm sorry, come again?'

'Well, you are part angel, aren't you?'

Rita was quiet for a long time after that.

The Magician stood within his chamber, hands flat against the sacrificial stone, the giant lump of grey rock on to which each woman had been chained, ready for the fall of the axe.

He could not sense Mr. Cotton, nor his brother, Mr. Spike.

'What's happened?' he asked.

'I do not know,' replied the Angel of Blackpool, and this sent a shiver through the Magician.

'How can you not know? You always know.'

'They are... hidden from me, should they choose to be, whilst in their own dream realm. They do not allow me into their house. Something must have happened to them.'

'I need them,' said the Magician, feeling weak and foolish.

'No,' replied the Angel, 'all that we require is each other, and we will always have that. Their job was done, anyway. The important part.'

The Magician straightened up, feeling a little better. 'If they're missing, then it's up to me.'

'Yes,' replied the Angel. 'Mr. Cotton and Mr. Spike have served us well, but have failed to retrieve what we need.'

'The axe.'

'The artefact that will break down the doors to Heaven and allow us to take revenge on our cold, indifferent creator.'

The Magician knew what he had to do. It was time to step out of the shadows and take what was his.

For his dad.

For his mum.

For every single person who'd ever walked the face of the planet.

24

It was past midnight and DS Dan Waterson should have been in bed.

He tried to go home once he was off the clock, but had instead found himself driving around Blackpool aimlessly, unable to go home and climb into bed while the world was crumbling around him.

The door in the arcade stockroom, it had been there, he was sure of it. He'd gripped the bloody handle and shook it, for God's sake. But then it hadn't been there before it had been. It had just been a wall, like it was again now. He leaned his forehead against the steering wheel of his car and scrunched his eyes shut.

A sharp tap at the driver's side window made him jerk upright.

'You okay there, mate?'

Waterson turned to see a familiar uniformed officer bent over and looking through the window. Chris Farmer.

'Yup, fine, just... past my bedtime,' replied Waterson, pulling the key out of the ignition and stepping into the police station car park to join Chris.

'On lates, too, eh?' asked Chris. 'Hard lines.'

'Yeah. Actually, I'm off duty, strictly speaking, but you know how it is with some cases. They rattle around in there and won't let you rest.' He tapped his skull.

'Not me,' Chris replied. 'The minute I'm done, I'm done. Lock it up in the back room and check back on it in the morning.' He grinned good-naturedly and Waterson attempted to oblige in return, but by the look of Farmer's expression, didn't exactly pull it off.

'You sure you're okay?'

'Rabbit ears, does that mean anything to you?'

'Rabbit ears?'

'Yes.'

'Well, yeah. I mean… it means rabbit ears to me. The ears of rabbits.'

Waterson nodded and headed towards the station building.

'Get some kip, Waters, you need it.'

Waterson stopped and turned slowly. 'What did you call me?' but Chris Farmer was already away, hands in his pockets, a carefree whistle on his lips.

Waters.

Nobody ever called him that. He hated it. An Uncle, Uncle Fisher, used to call him that. Used to call him a lot of things. Waters reminded him of Uncle Fisher so he stopped anyone calling him it. Why would Chris Farmer call him—

Waters.

Waterson winced and shook his head. For a moment the world tilted and he had to lean against the wall, but as soon as it started it was over. Waterson straightened up and made his way into the station, filling up a plastic cup with water from the machine in reception, nodding at the officer manning the front counter, and heading up the stairs to his desk.

It was sparsely populated at this hour, just Annie Lark in the far corner, buried in paperwork. DCI Jenner looked like he was in his office, too; lights on but blinds drawn. Waterson sat behind his desk and finished the water, dropping the cup into the bin. He looked to the empty desk. The one no one worked at but he was sure someone had. He ran his hands over the paper he'd doodled rabbit ears on.

Waters.

Waterson stood up sharply, his chair tumbling back and crashing to the floor.

Annie Lark looked round from the other side of the room. 'You okay, Dan?'

'Someone... someone did use that desk!' he replied.

DCI Jenner's office door opened and he stepped out. 'What's the fuss out here?'

Waterson pointed at the empty desk again.

'Aren't you off the clock, Waters?' asked Jenner.

Waterson staggered back like he'd just been punched in the brain.

'Red hair!' he said.

DCI Jenner looked, understandably, confused. He turned to Annie Lark, who shrugged her shoulders.

'She had red hair. Loads of it.' Waterson grabbed the chair to the always-empty desk and shoved it at his boss. 'She had red hair and sat in this chair behind that desk and she was my partner.'

Jenner stopped the chair as it rolled towards him and began pushing it back to its desk. 'Who had red hair?'

Waterson opened his mouth to reply, but it wasn't quite there yet. It was almost in the open, if he just kept chasing it, he'd tease the whole thing out. He paced the office, arms outstretched, hands grasping. It was as though he were chasing a thread... a thread attached to an answer, a thread that—if he could only catch the end of it—would let him pull the whole bloody truth into view.

'I don't know. A woman! My partner, why don't I have a partner? I did have, I know I did, and she sat there and she had red hair and she called me "Waters" every bloody day because she knew it drove me mental. And the dreams, nightmares... there was stuff about nightmares and rabbit ears and masks and it was all there and then it was gone.'

Jenner frowned again and looked down at the always empty desk. 'Now you mention it... that does sound... familiar...' he winced and placed a palm on his temple.

'Yes!' said Waterson, face manic with delight. 'I'm not crazy, something's happened and we've all forgotten her. How could we forget her? How could I?'

'Forget who?' said a fearful-looking Annie Lark.

Waterson pulled out his mobile phone and began scrolling through the contacts, and then there it was. A name. A name he was sure hadn't been there the last time he looked. He strutted over to DCI Jenner and showed him the name on screen.

'Rita bloody Hobbes!' said Waterson.

Carlisle woke with a jolt.

He sat up on the threadbare couch and sniffed through his elegant nose.

'Big Pins,' he said, his voice a croak.

There was a bottle of water by his feet. He picked it up, unscrewed the cap, and drank the lot without pausing for breath.

Carlisle looked down at his open shirt, at the paleness of his chest, and feathered his fingers over the pink scar that shone like a neon light. He'd always been a fast healer. She'd retrieved him, clearly. Rita had retrieved his body from the home of Mr. Cotton and Mr. Spike, and given his life back to him.

Carlisle tried to stand, to push himself up onto his feet, but his arms wobbled and then gave out, causing him to slump back and gasp for air. He'd died several times in his long existence, and coming back to life never got any easier. His bones positively throbbed with pain. His eyes were stabbed by every light, every colour. His mind was a jangle of metal chimes caught in a strong wind.

But he was alive.

It made him uncomfortable, putting his life in the hands of another, especially the hands of someone like Rita Hobbes, but needs must on occasion. He'd made his way to their home and he'd gotten them to tell him the truth. People, even monsters, were always more willing to share when they were sure the person they were talking to was about to die at their feet.

Carlisle smiled, but the muscles in his face hurt, so he stopped.

It had been a gamble, but one worth taking. Of course, he'd had no idea whether the detective would be able to retrieve him without stumbling into a similar fate as his own, but sometimes a roll of the dice makes life all the more interesting.

Outside, sat with Formby the eaves, Rita Hobbes was trying to take in the news.

'You are clearly bullshitting me,' she said.

'I am not. I do not bullshit. Actually, that isn't true, but in this case I don't.'

'So I'm an angel?'

'No.'

Rita felt like wrapping her hands around Formby's thick bristly neck. 'You just said I was!'

'Well, you are.'

Rita let out a little scream.

'I mean to say, you are a bit. About 0.0003 percent of people are. Back in the day, angels used to come down here and fraternise, y'see. Like sailors on leave. Dirty sods.'

'So you're saying some great, great, great relative of mine did the nasty with an angel, and a bit of that DNA, or whatever, has been passed on to me?'

Formby nodded and pushed aside his empty glass to reach for Rita's, only to be met with a slap on his knuckles.

Rita picked up her drink and took a mouthful. 'Blimey. Bloody hell. This is huge. No, bigger than huge. Detective Rita Hobbes, angel.'

'A little bit angel.'

'More angel than you, sunshine.'

Formby spread his arms and nodded.

'Ha! Angel. A bloody angel. And Miss Havers at the children's home said I'd never amount to anything. Showed you, you saggy-faced old bitch.'

The door behind the bar opened and Carlisle walked out, slow and stiff.

'Carlisle,' said Rita, vaulting the bar to greet him.

'If you're looking for a thank you,' he said, 'don't bother. It was the least you could do.'

'You're welcome.'

Carlisle grimaced, then winced.

'Guess what?' said Rita.

'No.'

'I'm only a sodding angel. Ha!'

Rita had never seen such a look of honest surprise spread across Carlisle's face. She rather enjoyed it.

'I beg your pardon?'

'Well,' said Formby, shuffling over, Rita's abandoned pint glass in his hand, 'little bit angel, from a long way back. Not much use, other than being able to handle weapons fashioned in Heaven, of course.'

Carlisle frowned. 'The axe.'

Rita grinned and held it aloft. 'You know, it's thanks to this bad boy that you're stood there now. Completely twatted both of those mask-wearing freaks with it. You should have seen me, complete bad-ass.'

'I... delighted for you,' replied Carlisle, wincing as he lowered himself on to a bar stool.

'Still coming round, eh?' asked Formby.

'I will be fine given a little time. This is not my first death.'

Rita snatched her drink back from a grumbling Formby, and downed the remainder in one. 'Bloody part angel,' she said, sitting next to Carlisle at the bar.

'Congratulations,' he replied, in a way that suggested he meant no such thing. 'No doubt it was that element of your being that also befuddled the hex so.'

'A lot of surprising stuff has happened recently, but me being a teensy bit angelic? That's definitely top of the pile.'

It was at this point that Rita's mobile phone began to ring. Rita, Carlisle, and Formby looked to her coat pocket, blankly.

'I think that's my phone ringing,' she said.

'It would seem so,' replied Carlisle.

'So what should I do?'

'I'm no expert,' said Carlisle, 'but I believe people usually answer them.'

Rita reached into her pocket and gingerly retrieved her ringing phone.

A name flashed on screen.

Rita pressed Answer. 'Um, hello?' she said.

'Yeah, uh, hello. Hi. Is this… are you Rita Hobbes?'

'Maybe,' said Rita, heart beating like a speed metal band's double kick bass drum.

'This might sound weird, but… did we used to be partners?'

Rita smiled as she felt a tear race down her cheek.

25

It was close to three in the morning, the moon high, and Blackpool seafront was deserted.

'This is a bad idea,' said Carlisle, for perhaps the tenth time.

Rita pulled her car to a stop and killed the engine. 'It's Waterson, my friend, my partner.'

'And he should not know that you exist. As far as ordinary people like him are concerned, you do not.'

'We were best friends, for years. Isn't it just possible that some memory of me stayed lodged in there and he, I don't know, shook it free?'

Carlisle frowned. 'It is... possible, I suppose.'

Rita felt like a child on Christmas Eve. The hex, the stupid magic some murdering bastard in a goat mask had inflicted on her, had erased her from everyday life. The only chance to have it lifted being to, apparently, kill the person behind it. Rita wasn't a killer. She didn't think she was, anyway. She took criminals to prison. They didn't get the escape of death. They lived through their guilt with their liberty taken.

Hexed Detective

But then she'd never been hexed before.

Trapped, only "alive" in an Uncanny between world. Able to walk the streets like everyone else did, but only as a phantom. A dream forgotten once awake. Her full existence for the Magician's life, that was the only chance she had, according to Carlisle, and maybe she'd have found herself having to make that choice, but now? Now her best friend had called her and she was about to meet him for a chat on the beach. Maybe there would be another way, after all.

As she stepped out of the car, the cold biting at her, she rested her hand on the axe tucked into the belt of her trousers. Even through the material of her coat, she felt the tickle of the magic it held prickle her skin.

Carlisle let out a muffled noise as he stiffly got out of the car and straightened up, joints cracking.

'Are you sure you're up for this?' asked Rita. 'I've got the axe. I'm okay.'

'No, you are not. If anything happens and you lose that axe, then I will be very upset. So if you insist on this foolhardy venture, it will be with me at your back.'

'Aw, I'm starting to think you only love me for what I've got in my pants,' said Rita, patting the axe as Carlisle frowned. 'Come on,' she said, nodding for him to follow as she started towards the steps leading down to the beach itself.

As the two stepped onto the sand, Carlisle narrowed his eyes at the distant sea, pulled away by the moon. 'God, I hate this place so,' he said.

'What was it like?' Rita asked.

'Be more specific, Detective,' replied Carlisle.

'Death. What was it like, being dead?'

'Like talking to you on Blackpool beach.'

Rita mimed hysterical laughter. 'Come on, Pasty, I'm serious. You were actually dead. Dead-dead. What was it like?

Can you remember? I mean, if there's a Heaven, then I'm assuming there's a place you go, so…'

Carlisle sighed but kept his eyes on the ocean. 'Death is different for different kinds of beings.'

'Well, what was it like for your kind of being?'

Carlisle frowned but did not reply as the wind toyed with the hem of his dark purple coat.

Rita sensed it best not to push the point any further. 'You still haven't said, by the way.'

'What I found out from Cotton and Spike?'

'You did find out something, right?'

Carlisle nodded. 'I did. I discovered whose hand is behind all of this.'

'The Magician? Well, who is it?'

'No. The power *behind* the Magician. The real power. There is a story, or a myth, or a lie, about a creature of pure darkness imprisoned beneath the waves. A creature that raged and screamed and fought against its bonds. Bonds fashioned in Heaven itself. The creature could not be cowed or killed, so a prison it had to be. It would seem that this creature, this horror, is a reality. That it lives and it has, at last, been able to influence an ally.'

'Well, crap. None of that sounds good.'

Carlisle smiled. 'No. It is very un-good indeed.'

'So what is it, exactly? This creature?'

'One of the original seven angels created by God to sit at His almighty side.'

'An angel? Like me?'

'You are not an angel.'

'I am a little bit.'

'My calling you an angel would be like saying this beach was an angel, because six grains of sand that lay upon it were actually skin cells from a passing celestial being.'

'Well, I'm still more angel than you are.'

'Most are,' replied Carlisle with a wry smile. The smile faltered. 'I believe he is here.'

Rita turned to see DS Waterson nervously approaching along the beach. She smiled and waved. Waterson raised a hand to return the wave, stopped, and shoved the un-waved hand into his coat pocket.

'Hey,' said Rita.

'Hi. Hello,' replied Waterson, his eyes drifting over to Carlisle, who was ignoring him, keeping his focus on the sea. 'Who's that?'

'A friend,' said Rita. 'Well, not a friend, a person. Sort of a person. He's someone I know.'

'Right.'

'It's... good to see you,' said Rita. 'And really good that you can see me. Obviously.' Rita felt daft, like she was sixteen and on a blind date.

'How is that you can remember her?' asked Carlisle.

'I don't know. I mean, I just remembered that I'd forgotten something. And it itched at me. And then, today, bang, there she was.'

'Bang, there I was,' said Rita, grinning.

'So, you were my partner?' asked Waterson.

'You don't know?' Rita replied.

'I know. I sort of know. It's all a bit foggy and unsure, but it's coming back to me, little by little. We were friends, right?'

Rita smiled. 'Best friends, Waters.'

'This is all very touching,' said Carlisle, 'but we actually have a case to solve. Impossible monsters to deal with. That sort of thing.'

'The case,' said Waterson. 'This case, with the women, what happened to you, it's something to do with the case, isn't it?'

'Okay,' said Rita, 'this is all gonna sound like madness

with a crazy side salad, but if you can accept that weird shit is definitely going on, then it's time we upgraded from Mulder and Scully to a pair of Mulders, right?'

'If you say so.'

Carlisle sighed and pinched the bridge of his nose. 'What has become of me? I once ruled a nation.'

'There's a magician, and a giant imprisoned angel, or something, and they're the ones taking and killing the women. Sacrificing them. Follow?'

'Follow,' replied Waterson.

'I got hexed saving Gemma Wheeler, and this hex—this magic—made me sort of disappear. No one could see me, or remember me.'

'Okay. Right. That is... a lot.'

'Yup.'

'So why are they doing all this? What's the point?'

'To get free, right?' said Rita, turning to Carlisle.

'In part. I imagine that is just step one, though.'

'So what's step two?' asked Rita.

'Perhaps your friend here, who can now conveniently both see and remember you, can fill us in on the remainder?'

Waterson shook his head. 'What are you talking about? All I know is what Rita's just told me.'

'How do I know you're not the secretive Magician in league with the Angel of Blackpool?' asked Carlisle.

'Carlisle, he's not evil, he's my friend,' said Rita.

'Luring this gullible wretch out into the open to finally dispatch her, take what is rightfully mine, so that you and the beast in the sea can complete your gambit? Answer me, boy!'

Dan Waterson opened his mouth to reply, then his eyebrows scrunched and his jaw moved soundlessly.

'Dan?' said Rita.

Waterson looked to her, confusion rippling across his face. He coughed, and red trickled down his chin.

'Shit, Dan, what's wrong with—'

Blood burst from Waterson's chest as a thick blade erupted through his rib cage.

'Waters!' said Rita, stumbling back in shock as his blood splattered her front.

As the blade was pulled back and disappeared from view, Waterson staggered forward, his hands catching on Rita's shoulders.

'Shit,' said Dan Waterson. 'Rita, I think I've been…' And then he fell to the ground, stone dead.

Where he had stood there was now a figure in scarlet robes and a goat mask, a bloodied blade in a leather-gloved hand. He ran the blade across his robes, wiping it clean of Dan Waterson's blood.

Rita was frozen, crouched by Waterson's lifeless body. 'Come on, Waters,' she said, rocking his shoulder with one hand. 'Stop playing silly beggars.'

Waterson didn't reply, didn't move.

'Magician,' said Carlisle.

The Magician took off his mask, with its winding goat horns, and Rita looked up to a familiar face.

'Hello, Rita,' said DCI Alexander Jenner.

26

Rita could still remember the first day she met Dan Waterson. The awkward early chats as they got to know each other as partners, as friends. The endless stake-outs, the mockery of each other's often disastrous love lives. The good times.

Now he was curled up on Blackpool beach, dead, his blood splattered across her front, her hands soaked in it.

'So you decided to step out of the shadows at last?' said Carlisle.

The Magician, DCI Alexander Jenner, smiled and nodded. 'What did you do to Cotton and Spike?' he asked.

'Would that I could claim responsibility, but I'm rather afraid that it was your erstwhile subordinate here that has, for the time being, sent them into hiding. Your muscle has deserted you. They are gone to lick their wounds.'

'They are just tools. Hands.' Jenner opened his palms and electricity, forks of orange fury, danced from finger to finger. 'I have access to a far greater power.'

Rita brushed aside tears, the blood on her hands smearing across her cheek. She stood, teeth clenching. 'You.

You killed those women.' She was repulsed to see something close to regret, to shame, move across Jenner's face.

'It was... necessary.'

Carlisle could feel the power, feel the magic that rolled invisibly around and through Jenner. Power like he'd never sensed before. He should abandon this folly. He was no hero, this was the detective's fight. He was weak, still too close to his death to fight at full tilt, and even if he hadn't been, this man, this magician, was tapping into magic far beyond his ken. He muttered a power word or two under his breath, and then he could see it. See a dark smoke trail that weaved lazily from Jenner and out across the waves.

An umbilical cord to the Angel of Blackpool.

The ageless, patient beast in its prison, feeding its strength to this mortal man. This ordinary thing without access to magic of his own. To the Uncanny world.

He should turn and run.

The Angel and the Magician, they wanted nothing from him. All they wanted was for their work to continue, and for that to happen they required the axe. They would take it, and they would most likely turn Rita Hobbes into a grim confetti.

But it was *his* axe.

His artefact.

How he ached at the thought of holding it again. For it to accept him. React to him. To give him everything his hungry heart demanded. He had been someone with that artefact. Someone more than the liar, the feared, the untrustworthy criminal.

And so he stayed.

'I see your connection to the Angel of Blackpool,' he said, and touched Rita's shoulder. Now she could see it too.

'We have a joint purpose. A great duty,' replied Jenner.

Rita looked, wide-eyed, at the black smoke that coiled

and weaved around DCI Jenner. That stretched from him and away across the sea.

'You have no magic in you,' said Carlisle. 'You are nothing. Less than nothing. A duped fool. A hapless tool.'

Jenner stepped forward, fury twisting his face. 'No! I am *someone*. I am *important*! I will make God Himself tremble!'

Carlisle snorted contemptuously. 'And people say that *I* am full of myself.'

Rita threw her coat open and pulled the axe from where it hung against her leg. 'This what you want, is it?' she said, her voice a snarl.

'Be careful,' said Carlisle, the ache in his stomach throbbing, pushing him to make a useless grab for the axe. He resisted.

'Well,' said Rita, 'isn't this what you need to carry on your "necessary" work?'

'Give it to me.' Jenner reached for the axe and Rita stepped back.

'If you want it, you murdering piece of shit, you're gonna have to take it from me. And the only way you're gonna do that is if I'm dead.'

'Okay then.' Jenner's eyes turned oil-slick black.

Carlisle felt the change in the air around them. Saw the smoky umbilical cord thicken, become denser, as more power was fed from prison to man.

'I see a dusting of Heaven on you,' came a voice from Jenner's mouth. It was not the voice of Jenner himself. It was rich and thick and it made Rita's hands tremble.

'We are now speaking with the Angel of Blackpool, I presume?' asked Carlisle.

'Hexed and hunted and attacked, and yet still she persists,' said the Angel, almost, it seemed to Rita, in admiration.

'Yeah, I'm annoying like that,' she said.

'And in countless other ways,' added Carlisle.

The world around them began to shimmer.

'Look,' said Rita, pointing out to sea. A great shadow hung over the ocean in the distance. A shape. A hulking, writhing beast. A thing of horror that made Rita's mind want to retreat. Want to deny.

'Perhaps we can speak in person,' said the Angel, and Jenner reached out to touch both Rita and Carlisle.

The world shuddered and moved out of focus, and the sound of the beast gibbering in a million forgotten tongues filled the air.

And then silence.

Rita opened her eyes to find herself in a cold, vaulted chamber. Giant marble columns thicker than ancient redwoods stretched from floor to ceiling all around them, and millions of candles flickered, lighting the place. The space was perfectly silent, as though a sound had not been made within its walls for centuries.

'What is this? A church? A crypt?' asked Rita.

'No,' replied Carlisle, 'a prison.'

He strode forward, Rita catching up, their footfalls on the stone floor echoing. They rounded a column and found the Angel of Blackpool.

27

It stood inside a glass box and wore brilliant white robes. It had an easy smile upon its face, and its hair was thick and golden. It was the most beautiful thing Rita had ever seen.

'God could have provided a chair, at the very least,' said Carlisle, and the Angel laughed. It sounded to Rita like songbirds.

'Where is this?' she asked.

'Under the ocean,' replied the Angel, 'and between reality and reality and reality. Folded away. Forgotten. Ignored.'

'Well, that clears that up,' said Rita.

The Angel unleashed its songbird laughter once again. 'What have you done to my friends, Mr. Cotton and Mr. Spike, I wonder?'

'What's wrong, aren't they picking up the phone?' asked Carlisle.

The Angel looked troubled, just for a moment.

'Ah, a limit to your power,' said Carlisle. 'You can't reach into their dreamscape, can you?'

Hexed Detective

The Angel turned its attention to Rita, who felt the warmth of its gaze. 'I had wondered why the artefact accepted you,' he said, 'and now I know. A weapon of Heaven, in the hands of the divine.'

'You should see me when I've had time to do my makeup properly.'

'You did not know of your ancestry for such a long time. Another of the creator's ignored flock. Tell me, what was it like to grow up alone, without family, with people paid to care? People who could not hide that they did not?'

'Ignore it,' said Carlisle. 'It is trying to get its hooks into you.'

'Carlisle,' said the Angel, 'I have often heard whispers of you. Oh, the things you have done, and yet you would judge me?'

'I judge everyone. It's sort of my thing,' he replied, grinning. 'Tell me, you've been imprisoned here for millennia, silent and alone—'

'So how did I make a connection with Alexander Jenner?' the Angel cut in.

Carlisle bowed his head.

The Angel smiled. 'It took… patience. Effort. Have you ever heard the story of the bird that sharpened its beak on the diamond mountain, until, after an eternity, the entire mountain was chiselled away?'

'No,' said Rita. 'I'm more of a soap opera girl, myself.'

'I tapped, and I tapped, and I tapped,' said the Angel, 'and finally, a little of myself broke through. Just a little, but enough. I reached out and found a sad little boy, wronged by God, and we became… friends.'

'Having to reach out to a mortal for help, you must have been desperate,' said Carlisle.

A snarl broke the Angel's beauty as it bashed its fists

against its glass cage and the candlelight shook, casting nightmare shadows around the chamber.

'Do not mock me, thief.'

'You stand there, a thing of beauty, but that is not the real you,' said Carlisle. 'We saw the true shape of your soul out there as we stood upon the beach. A thing of endless horror, casting a shadow of despair.'

The Angel's breathing slowed and it regained its composure. 'What you see as horror, I see as splendour. For what is a being realising its full potential if not a thing of beauty?'

'Why have you brought us here?' asked Rita.

'Yes, I was rather wondering that myself.'

'I had hoped to appeal to your better judgment, Rita Hobbes.'

'Oh, right, then go right ahead, mate.'

'You have suffered, as have I.'

'I've had a few knocks along the way, yeah.'

'You, part angel, and yet still punished by a creator who does not care for your pain. Your anguish. You fight against me, but I am not your enemy.'

'That right, is it?'

'You believe in justice.'

Rita looked at him with hooded eyes. 'Yeah. So?'

'Then help me get it. For myself. For Alexander Jenner. For yourself. For the whole of existence that has stood cold as its creator turned His back upon them. Every day, children die and nobody cares. The innocent become sick and suffer slow, agonising deaths. Hurricanes sweep up unopposed and crash against the living, leaving anguish in their wash.'

Rita stepped closer to the glass cage.

'Rita,' said Carlisle, reaching out, but she batted his hand aside.

The Angel spoke. 'The elderly are abandoned and abused

Hexed Detective

and He *does. Not. Care.* He is the true monster, and He must face the consequences of His inaction.'

'My life. My life has been His fault?'

'From conception to now. It could have been different.'

'It *should* have been.'

'Rita…' said Carlisle.

'Well, It's right, in a way, isn't It?'

The Angel smiled.

'No, It's not. It's evil.'

'But then what does that make God?'

Carlisle shrugged. 'An arsehole?'

'The fear, the loneliness,' said Rita, 'feeling always unwanted and in the way. That was my childhood.'

'Yes, I know the sob story,' replied Carlisle.

'You see, you understand,' the Angel told Rita.

'Yeah, I think I understand. And you know what I think?' asked Rita.

'What?'

Rita pressed her palms against the glass cage and grinned. 'I think you're so full of shit it's a wonder you're not drowning in there.'

Carlisle smirked, then caught himself. 'My apologies. Well, it was lovely to drop in for a visit. We really mustn't do it again some time. Detective, let us take our leave.'

'Sounds good to me.'

'You shall not leave,' said the Angel.

'Oh, we shall,' replied Carlisle.

'I do not allow it.'

'Not big on being told what to do, mate,' said Rita.

'I am taking us out of this sad place to another, well, very sad place,' said Carlisle.

'Aren't we going back to Blackpool?'

'Indeed.'

'Oh. Right. Good one.'

'You are weak,' said the Angel. 'You have little power in you now. A strong wind would bend you double.'

'True, but I always make sure I have a card up my sleeve.'

Carlisle reached into his coat and pulled out a small pouch tied with string. 'Rita!' he grabbed her hand as the Angel raged within its glass cage. Carlisle knew this would cost him—that the effort would bring him to his knees—but he would have to take the risk.

'Is that a bomb?' asked Rita.

'Quiet, fool,' replied Carlisle.

'Oh, very nice.'

Carlisle gathered up as much magic as his body could stand—his every nerve-ending screaming in agony—and muttered the incantation. He threw the pouch at the ground as the Angel began screaming in a million ancient languages, and the prison whipped from view. The world around them tumbled and twirled, but he held tight to Rita's hand as she screamed, because if he let go, she might be lost forever. Finally, the whirl of reality slowed and they fell to the ground.

'Holy shit…' said Rita, sitting up.

Carlisle attempted to push himself up, the pain excruciating.

Rita rolled onto her knees and helped him up. 'Are you okay?'

'I'm fine,' he replied, sharply, then sagged. 'I'm not fine. It is too soon since my death, and that spell… that was some extreme magic.'

Sweat dripped from Carlisle's pale face. The whites of his eyes were now blood-red.

'You're not going to die again, are you?'

Carlisle chuckled, then regretted it as his chest screamed in agony. 'I am afraid not, Detective, but the life in me is weak, the magic weaker, still. We must retreat to safety until I can regain my strength.'

Rita stood, helping Carlisle up to his feet. 'Can you walk?' she asked.

'Yes, I can walk,' Carlisle replied, though he wasn't sure how true that was.

Rita looked around to see where they'd ended up, and recognised the entrance to the Night Fair behind them. Carlisle's magic hadn't taken them far.

'So, we just had a chat with an evil angel?' said Rita.

'Indeed.'

'Well, they always say you can judge a person by the quality of their enemies.'

'They do.'

'And that thing is a shitting doozy. So well done us, I say.'

'You are a blithering fool, Detective.'

'Yes, I am,' she replied, grinning.

Carlisle took an experimental step forward and was delighted to find that his legs did not betray him.

'So, any ideas?' asked Rita.

'Always.'

'Okay, Mister Big Head, care to share?'

'The Magician, your erstwhile boss, is connected to the Angel of Blackpool.'

'The smoke thing?' asked Rita, recalling the umbilical cord of black smoke that had stretched from Jenner and out over the ocean.

'That is what is feeding magic, feeding power, to the Magician.'

'Then we've gotta find a way to cut the cord.'

'Precisely.'

'Okay, how'd we do that?'

He smiled and turned to Rita.

'We must—' began Carlisle, but his words cut off as a ball of fire struck him, and his body shot back and away.

Rita reached out to him, calling his name, but he was gone. She looked up to see Alexander Jenner, scarlet robes billowing, floating towards her within a corona of flames, his eyes still ink-black.

28

'What did you do?' shouted Rita, axe gripped in her hands.

'I asked nicely. Now I will take,' replied the Angel within its Jenner puppet.

'Come on then you big… idiot!' Rita had hoped for bolder words, but that would have to do.

Jenner's face smiled and he rubbed his hands together, great swirls of purple and yellow and blue crackling to life.

'Time to die, Detective.' He punched out a hand and the magic burst from it.

Rita leapt to one side as it struck the spot where she had been standing. Not pausing to look back, she rolled onto her feet and ran for the Night Fair's gate, only to find it locked. 'Great, a Night Fair that closes when it's actually night.'

'There is nowhere to run to, Detective. Nowhere to hide. Not anymore. The end is here and the work must continue. God must be punished.'

Rita fell backwards just in time to doge another blast of lethal magic, which smashed into the gates, blowing them apart.

'Thanks!'

She raced through the shattered gates and into the Night Fair, darting from path to path between empty stalls, always taking the next turn, trying not to give Jenner, or the Angel piloting him, a clear line of sight. Not that this stopped it from continuing to attack, as spell after spell erupted from his hands and stalls burst into flames all around her.

'Shit, shit, shit,' said Rita, looking back over her shoulder and seeing Jenner floating into view, eyes pitch-black, a serene smile upon his face.

'I believe I will kill you slowly,' said the Angel through Jenner.

'No thanks,' replied Rita, right before she found herself at a dead end. 'Oh, bollocks.'

She turned, grasping the axe as Jenner in his corona of flames hovered into view, blocking any escape. 'DCI Jenner, please, listen to me,' she cried.

The ground a few feet in front of her exploded, showering her with dirt.

'Come on, you're in there, you're a good man, you don't need to carry on with this.'

Light burst from Jenner's hand and Rita instinctively swung out with the axe, connecting with the oncoming magic.

She felt its purpose roll through her. Magic meant to destroy. To hurt. To decimate. It was hers now, and as she swung the axe again, she sent it back to where it had come from. It shot from the axe head as she screamed and struck Jenner in the chest, sending him flying backwards as if he was tied to a bungee cord.

'Eat shit,' she cried, then ran back the way she'd came, escaping the dead end.

She wasn't helpless. This axe gave her power. Power to capture and control magic, to understand it and turn it against the person who would use it against her. Rita smiled, almost laughed. She wasn't going to carry on running. Dan Waterson was dead, and the person responsible for that was in here, in the Night Fair, with her, and she was going to do her damnedest to bring him to justice.

'Hey, big scary Angel, where are you? Come to mamma.' Rita sounded brave, but her stomach still churned and her heart beat-beat-beat.

She whirled round to see Jenner walking towards her.

'Oh, decided to stop the flying bit, have you?' she asked.

'You are alone,' he said, the Angel's voice emerging from Jenner's mouth.

'A girl is never alone with a chip on her shoulder and a magic hatchet in her hands,' she replied, raising the weapon, ready to fend off whatever came her way.

Jenner just smiled.

'You can repel an attack or two, perhaps even three, but I will get you. Beat you down. It's just a question of time, and I am immortal. I have all the time in existence.'

He flung another ball of crackling magic at her and Rita gasped, swinging at it, taking control of it, and sending it back in the direction it came from. But Jenner, the Angel, was ready this time, and casually swatted the returned magic aside.

A food stand burst into flames. He was right. *It* was right. But Rita had no intention of standing her ground and seeing how many balls she could hit before she was out.

'The Magician, your erstwhile boss, is connected to the Angel of Blackpool.'

'The smoke thing?'

'That is what is feeding magic. Feeding power to the Magician.'

'So we've gotta find a way to cut the cord.'

She flexed her fingers around the hilt of the axe and searched for it. Called to it. Demanded it did as she wished.

There it was.

More magic flew at her, thrown contemptuously, and she returned it with a cry of effort.

Mr. Cotton and Mr. Spike, hidden in their dreamscape. That was her one hope. Her one chance.

'I have toyed with you long enough,' said the Angel.

Rita ignored It.

Instead, she began to speak with the axe, not in words, but in thoughts, in feelings, in understanding.

It held the magic still.

The magic she had taken when she struck Mr. Spike.

The magic she had not yet used.

It was dark magic, she could sense that. Magic from a bleak place of nightmares and pain. And it was hers to use.

The Angel lifted Jenner's arms and a storm of angry power swarmed around him. Flames burst into life and he floated once more, levitating slowly into the air. He was laughing. That birdsong laugh, but it no longer sounded beautiful. It sounded wrong. It sounded cruel.

It was almost the end. But not in the way the Angel had expected.

Rita spoke with her axe, with the dark magic that raged within. She soothed it and it responded to her request.

It built a prison.

The flames around Jenner's body died in an instant, and he dropped to the ground, crashing to his hands and knees in surprise.

'It's over,' said Rita.

He looked up at her with wide, confused eyes. The eyes were no longer ink-black. 'What... wh-what have you done?' he asked in his own voice, his actual voice, not the Angel's.

'I've done my job,' replied Rita. 'I've caught the murderer

and put him away.' She walked slowly towards him, and Jenner fell back onto his rear, scrambling away from her, terrified, until his back struck the side of a stall. He looked around, confused.

'Yeah, still the Night Fair,' said Rita. 'Well, sort of. It's not the actual Night Fair. This is one me and the axe here made.'

'I don't... I don't understand...'

'I took Mr. Spike's magic, or a piece of it, anyway, and that pair, they can create little, like, dreamscapes. Little places cut off from the real world. So that's what I did. Quicker just to copy where we were in the first place. Now this is all there is for you. This Night Fair. There isn't anything past the fences, past the gate. Just this place.'

'Angel?' said Jenner, grabbing the edge of the stand's counter and pulling himself to his feet. 'Angel, talk to me. Please, talk to me!'

Rita almost felt sorry for him, he looked so pathetic.

Almost.

'It can't hear you. Can't get to you. It's reach doesn't extend into here, into a dreamscape, I'm afraid, Guv. The blabbermouth thing sort of let that slip. Careless, eh? But then arrogant twats like that always say more than they should. Can't help themselves.'

Jenner fell back to the dirt, tears streaming down his face. 'No... no... I need it... it's not in my head anymore, not in my head...'

'And neither is your connection to magic,' she said, crouching by him. 'That was all the Angel, now it's just you again. Sorry. Well, not sorry. Not at all, really.'

'You don't understand, I'm a good man.'

'And how do you work that one out, genius?'

'We were going to punish God. For killing my mum. My dad. He deserves it.' Jenner made a grab for Rita, but she struck him on the forehead with the butt of the axe and he stumbled to the ground face-first, blood streaming from his forehead. He rolled onto his back, crying.

'Angel... please... talk to me... help me...'

'Those women. Dan Waterson. You're guilty, and this is where you'll rot. Hey, now you've got a prison, and your crazy Angel pal has a prison. Nice how that balances out, isn't it?'

Rita stood and walked to the Night Fair's gate.

'You can't leave me in here!'

'I bloody well can, Guv.'

And she walked out of the gate, back into the real world.

29

Rita was lining up a ball, one eye closed, scoping out the pins at the end of the aisle, when Carlisle walked through the door of the bowling alley and joined her.

'So you're not dead?' he noted.

'You neither,' replied Rita, then rolled the ball, swinging out her right leg for balance. It shot down the aisle and cleared the pins in one.

'Get in!' she said, giving herself a celebratory fist pump.

Rita turned and sat opposite Carlisle, taking a sip of her drink. She could feel Carlisle's eyes on the axe as it dangled from her belt.

'What happened to you then?' she asked.

'Knocked out for a few hours. And how about you?'

'Just closed the case. Bad guy locked up. Connection to evil angel severed. And all was well in the world. Or in Blackpool at least. For a bit.'

'You are still hexed.'

Rita frowned, then shrugged and took another sip from her ale.

'So the Magician is not dead?' asked Carlisle.

'I'm not a killer,' she replied.

'Then where is he?'

'In prison. Safe from the Angel's magic.'

'I asked where?'

'I told you. Prison.'

Carlisle stared down his nose at her. 'Then you will remain in this state, trapped in Blackpool and hidden from the ordinary world.'

'Seems so.'

'I could kill him for you.'

'Yeah, but I'm not sure I'm cool with that, either. I want him to serve his time. His life sentence. That's justice.'

Carlisle snarled and swept the glasses from the table. 'We had a deal.'

'I'm sorry,' she replied. 'I can't just… he was being used. Influenced. Pushed. Ever since he was a kid.'

'Oh, so he lives because of what? Diminished responsibility?'

'Yeah. If you like. That thing, that Angel, used him. He deserves justice, he doesn't deserve death.'

'That artefact is mine. Give it to me.'

Rita placed her hand protectively on the butt of the axe. 'I can't.'

Carlisle flinched towards her, his face a mask of anger, and for a second, she thought he might attack her. 'It belongs to me,' he said through clenched teeth. 'I helped you. I died for you. It is my property.'

Rita dropped her head then looked up at Carlisle, into his fierce eyes. 'Until I know how to get out of all of this, I need it. It's staying with me.' She gripped the axe's hilt. 'So, will you help me?'

Carlisle straightened out his dark purple coat, then turned on his heel and walked out of Big Pins. Rita sagged back and blew, trying to get rid of the tension.

Hexed Detective

Formby shuffled over from a corner and joined her. 'May I?' he asked.

'Sure.'

Formby took her drink and downed it.

'I thought you meant, "May I sit down?" but okay.'

'You might have made yourself a bit of an enemy in Carlisle, Detective,' said Formby, scratching at his round, stubbled face.

'He'll come around,' she said. She wasn't sure she believed herself, though.

'And the Angel. You cut off its access to the Magician, but don't think that'll be that.'

Rita waved until she caught Linton's attention. 'Two pints here, mate.'

Linton gave a little salute and got to it.

'Then maybe that's what I've got to do. Take down an angel gone bad. It wasn't Jenner's magic that even did this to me, the hex. It was the Angel's magic. Maybe… maybe if I stop the Angel, the hex will go away, and I can go back to my life.'

'Maybe. Wasn't much of a life to start with, though, was it?'

'Oi! It was okay.'

'I hear lots, remember,' he said, exposing his piranha teeth with a big grin.

'Charming. You know, it was okay, actually. Bits of it. Sometimes.'

'Really?'

Rita stuck her tongue out at Formby, and took her pint from Linton. She'd wanted something different. Something new. Anything new. And yeah, maybe she was stuck, literally, in Blackpool, but hadn't she got her wish? Sort of? Okay, it wasn't ideal, but what in life is?

Rita sat back and patted her magic axe as she sipped a

pint within a bowling alley that catered to monsters and the magical.

Yeah.

This was certainly different to her usual.

The Angel sat with its legs crossed on the floor of its glass prison, and it concentrated.

It tapped. It tapped. It tapped.

This was just a minor setback.

It would take time, but more chances would come.

Yes, all it would take was time.

And the Angel of Blackpool had all of eternity on its side.

LEAVE A REVIEW

Reviews are gold to indie authors, so if you've enjoyed this book, please consider visiting the site you purchased it from and leaving a quick review.

BECOME AN INSIDER

Sign up and receive **FREE UNCANNY KINGDOM BOOKS**. Also, be the **FIRST** to hear about **NEW RELEASES** and **SPECIAL OFFERS**. Just visit:

WWW.UNCANNYKINGDOM.COM

ALSO SET IN THE UNCANNY KINGDOM

The Hexed Detective Series
Hexed Detective
Fatal Moon
Night Terrors

The Uncanny Ink Series
Bad Soul
Bad Blood
Bad Justice
Bad Intention
Bad Thoughts
Bad Memories

The London Coven Series
Familiar Magic
Nightmare Realm
Deadly Portent
Other London

Also Set in the Uncanny Kingdom

The Spectral Detective Series
Spectral Detective
Corpse Reviver
Twice Damned
Necessary Evil
Deadly Departed

The Dark Lakes Series
Magic Eater
Blood Stones
Past Sins

The Branded Series
Sanctified
Turned
Bloodline

The Myth Management Series
Myth Management

Copyright © 2018 by Uncanny Kingdom.

All rights reserved.

No part of this book may be reproduced in any form or by any electronic or mechanical means, including information storage and retrieval systems, without written permission from the author, except for the use of brief quotations in a book review.

Printed in Great Britain
by Amazon